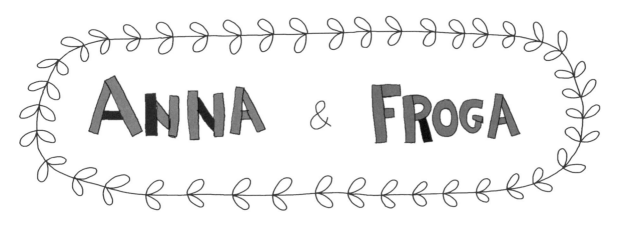

ANNA & FROGA

Want a gumball?

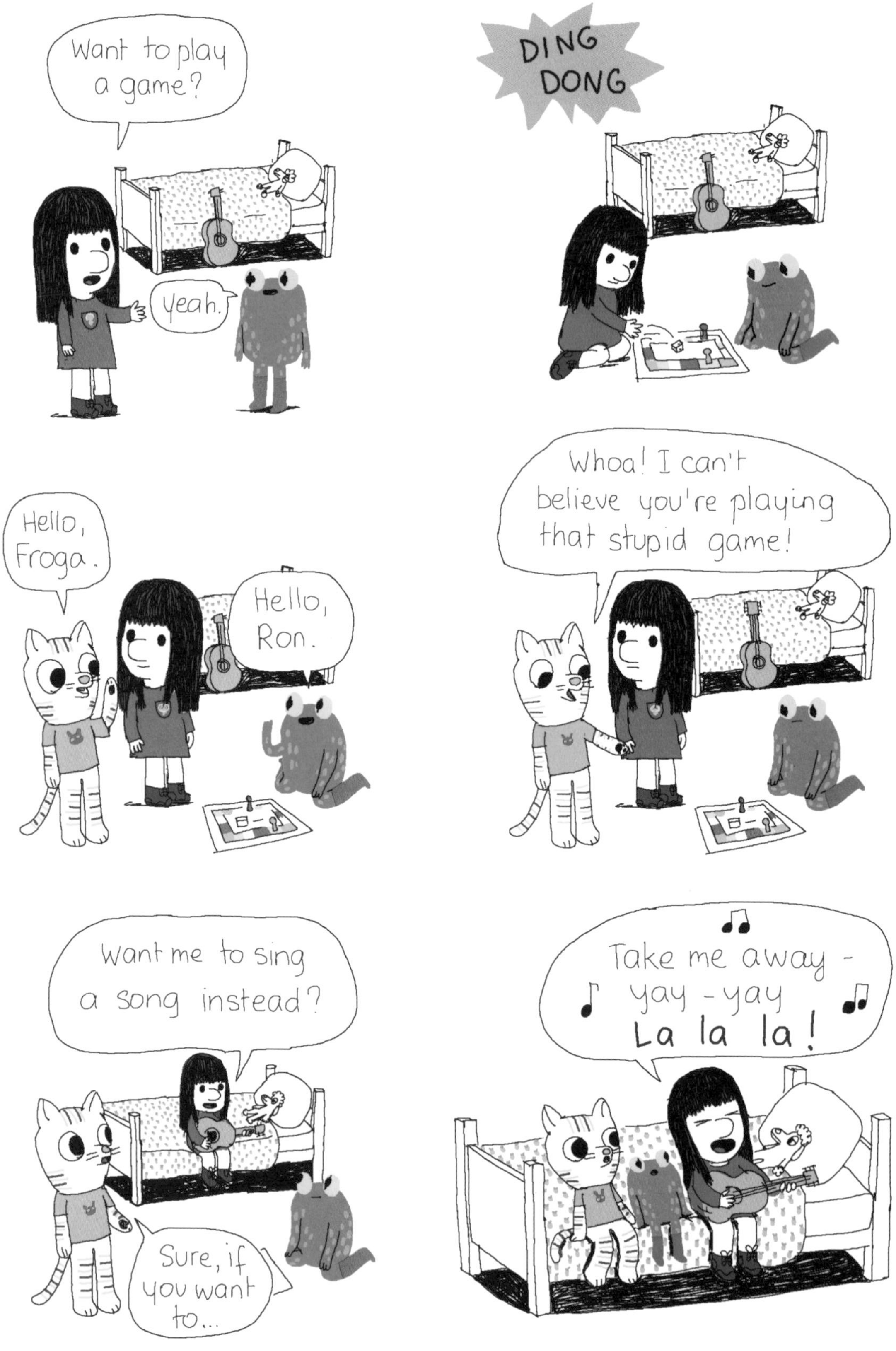
Want to play a game?
Yeah.
DING DONG
Hello, Froga.
Hello, Ron.
Whoa! I can't believe you're playing that stupid game!
Want me to sing a song instead?
Sure, if you want to...
Take me away - yay - yay
La la la!

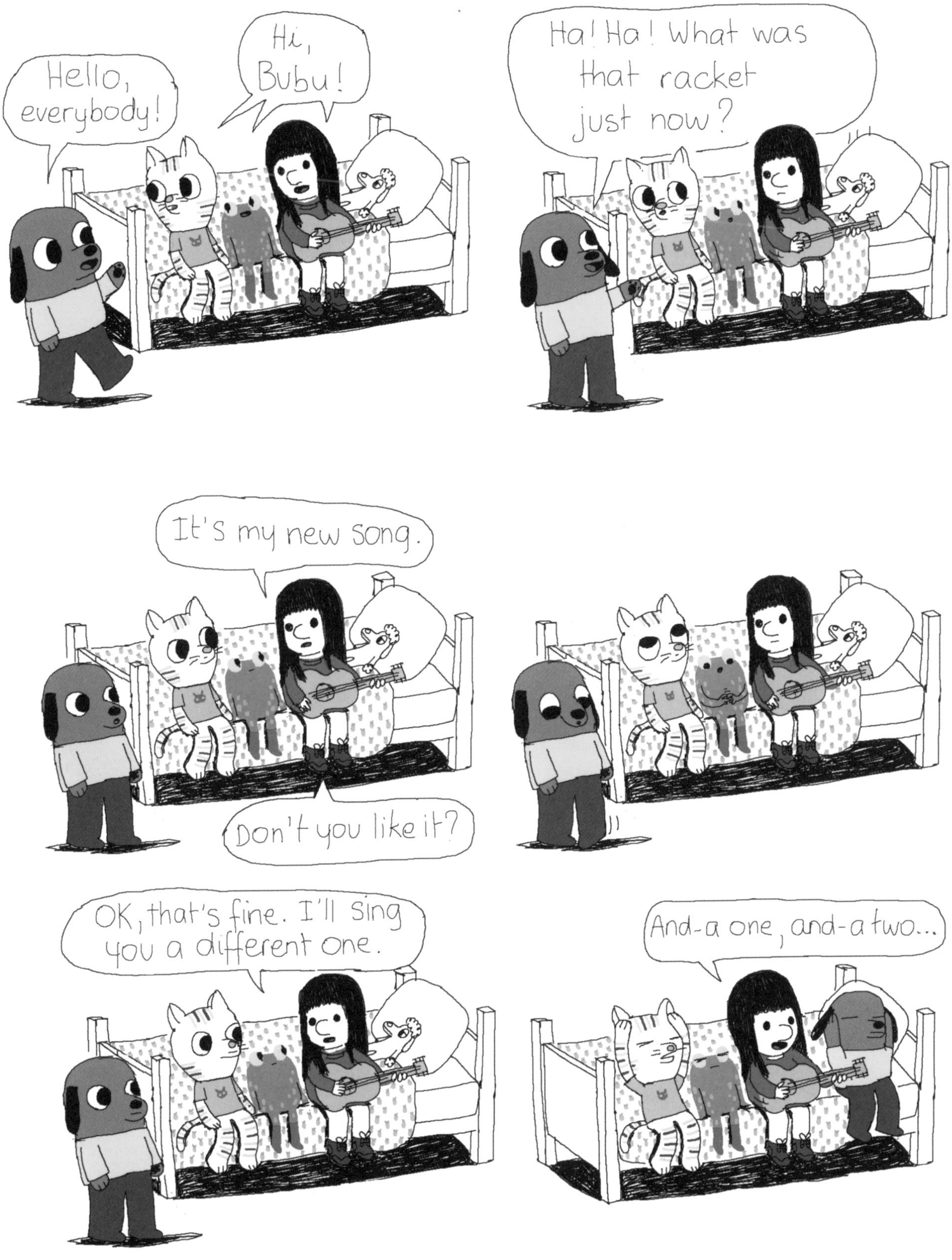
Hello, everybody!
Hi, Bubu!
Ha! Ha! What was that racket just now?
It's my new song.
Don't you like it?
OK, that's fine. I'll sing you a different one.
And-a one, and-a two...

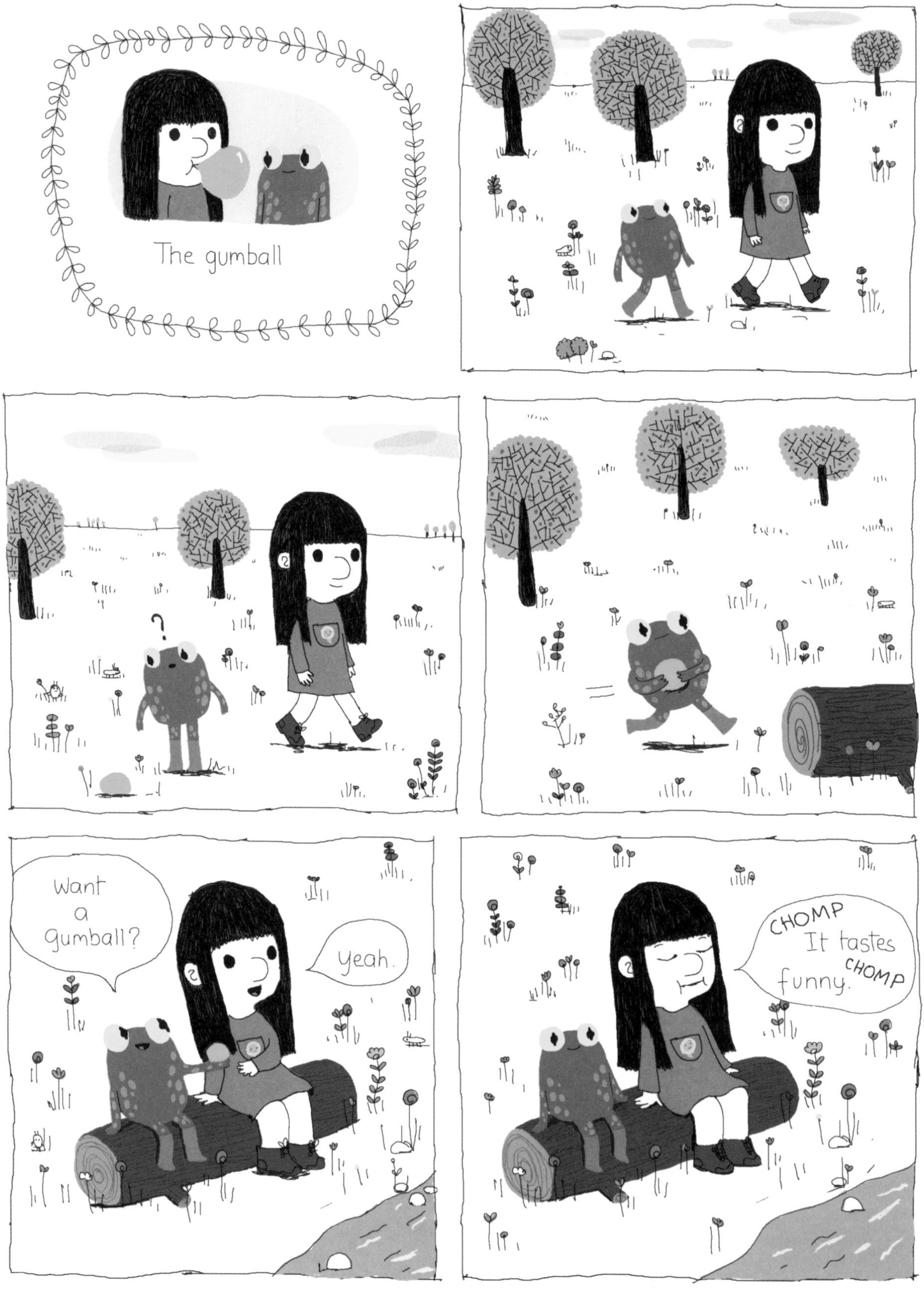
The gumball
?
Want a gumball?
Yeah.
CHOMP It tastes CHOMP funny.

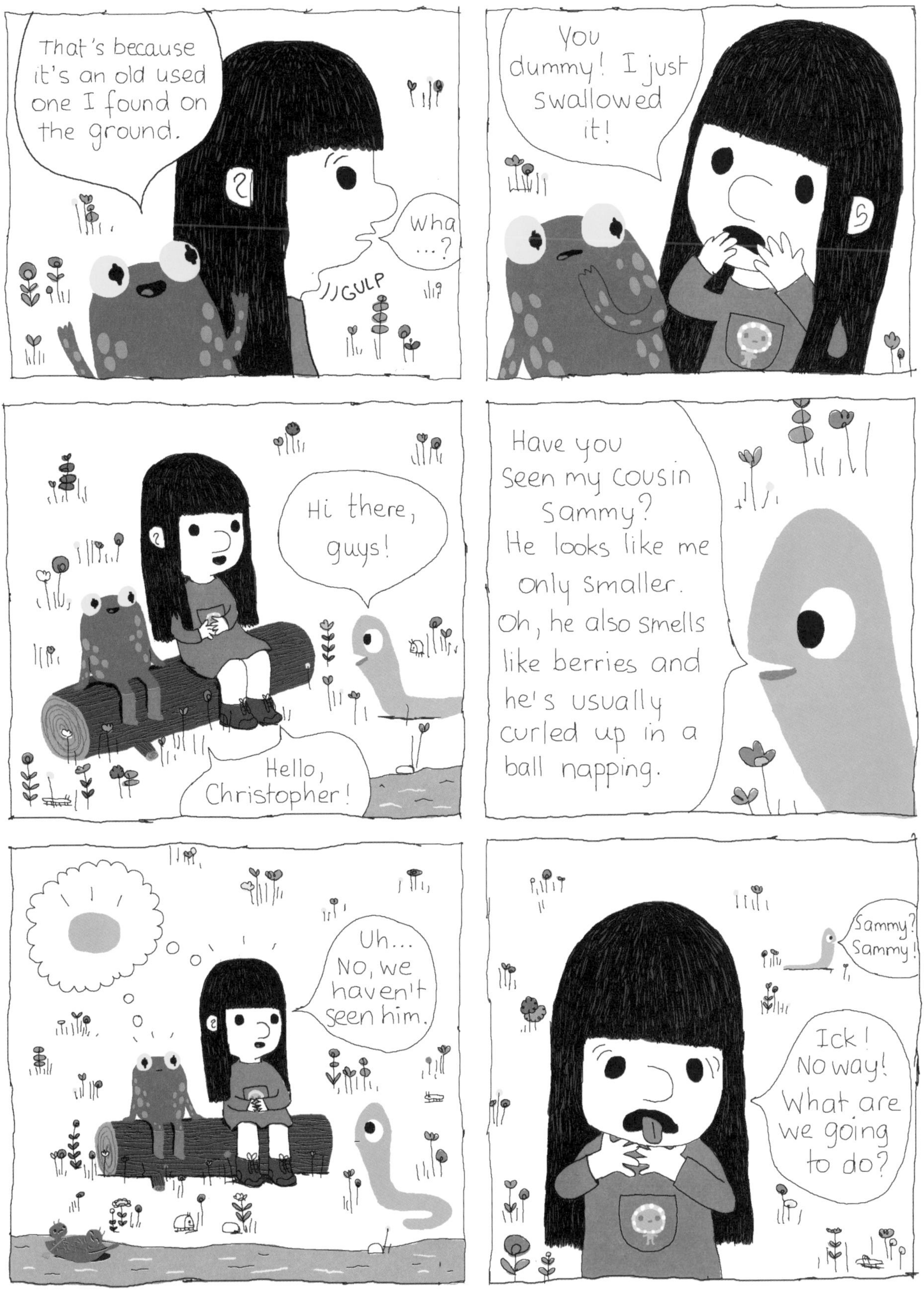
That's because it's an old used one I found on the ground.
GULP
Wha ...?
You dummy! I just swallowed it!
Hi there, guys!
Hello, Christopher!
Have you seen my cousin Sammy? He looks like me only smaller. Oh, he also smells like berries and he's usually curled up in a ball napping.
Uh... No, we haven't seen him.
Sammy? Sammy!
Ick! No way! What are we going to do?

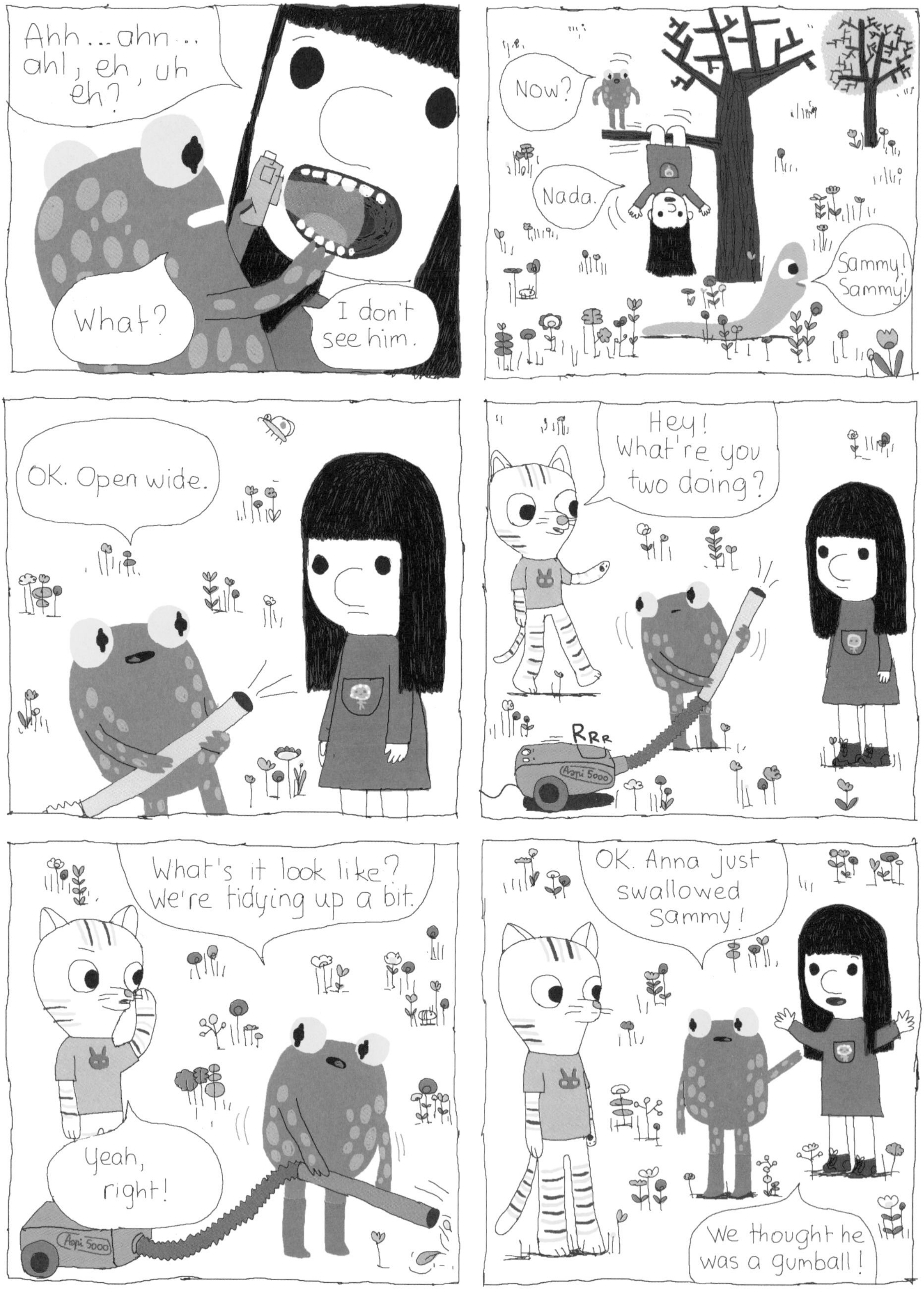
Ahh...ahn... ahl, eh, uh eh?
What?
I don't see him.
Now?
Nada.
Sammy! Sammy!
OK. Open wide.
Hey! What're you two doing?
RRR
What's it look like? We're tidying up a bit.
Yeah, right!
OK. Anna just swallowed Sammy!
We thought he was a gumball!

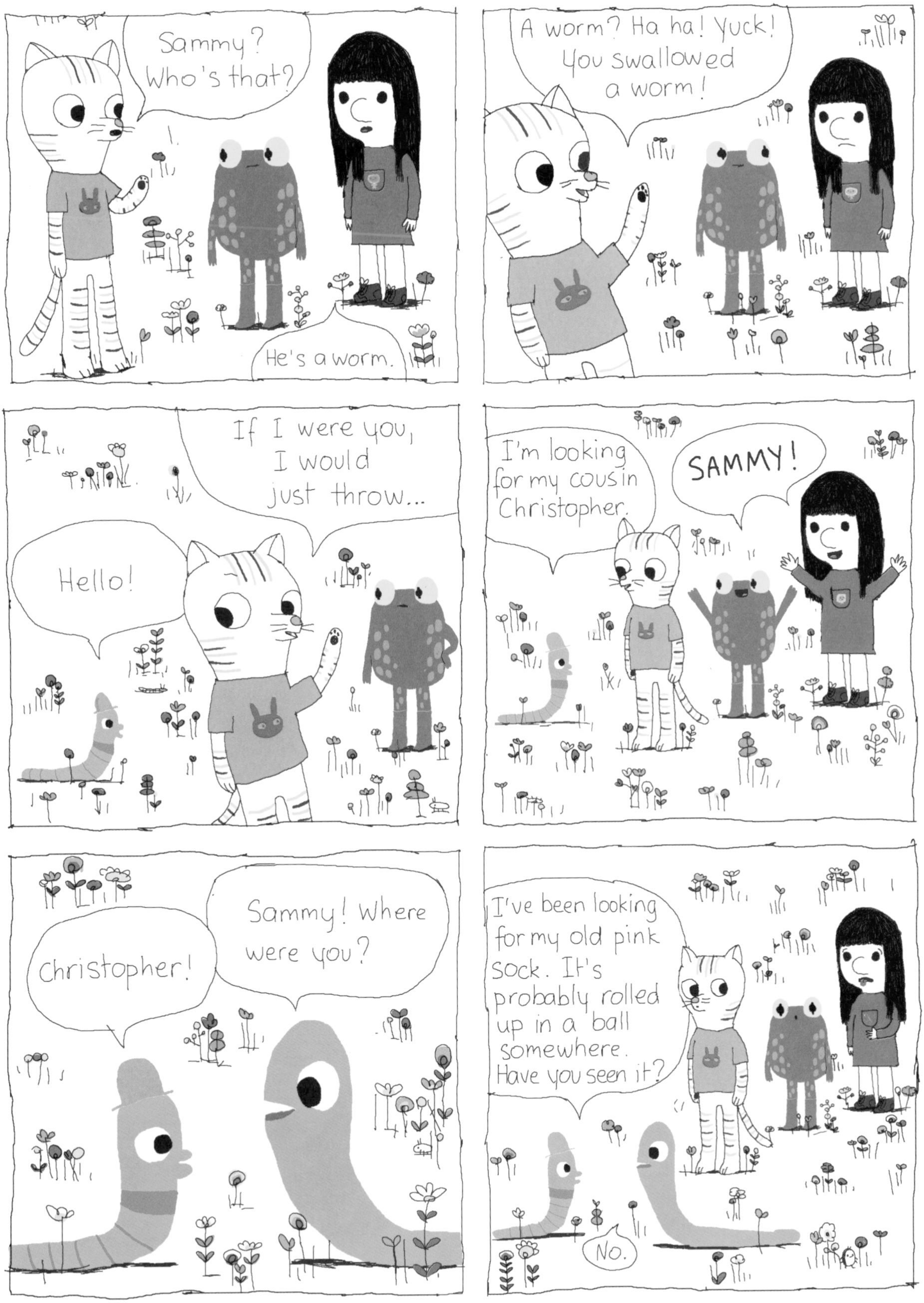

Sammy? Who's that?
He's a worm.
A worm? Ha ha! Yuck! You swallowed a worm!
If I were you, I would just throw...
Hello!
I'm looking for my cousin Christopher.
SAMMY!
Christopher!
Sammy! Where were you?
I've been looking for my old pink sock. It's probably rolled up in a ball somewhere. Have you seen it?
No.

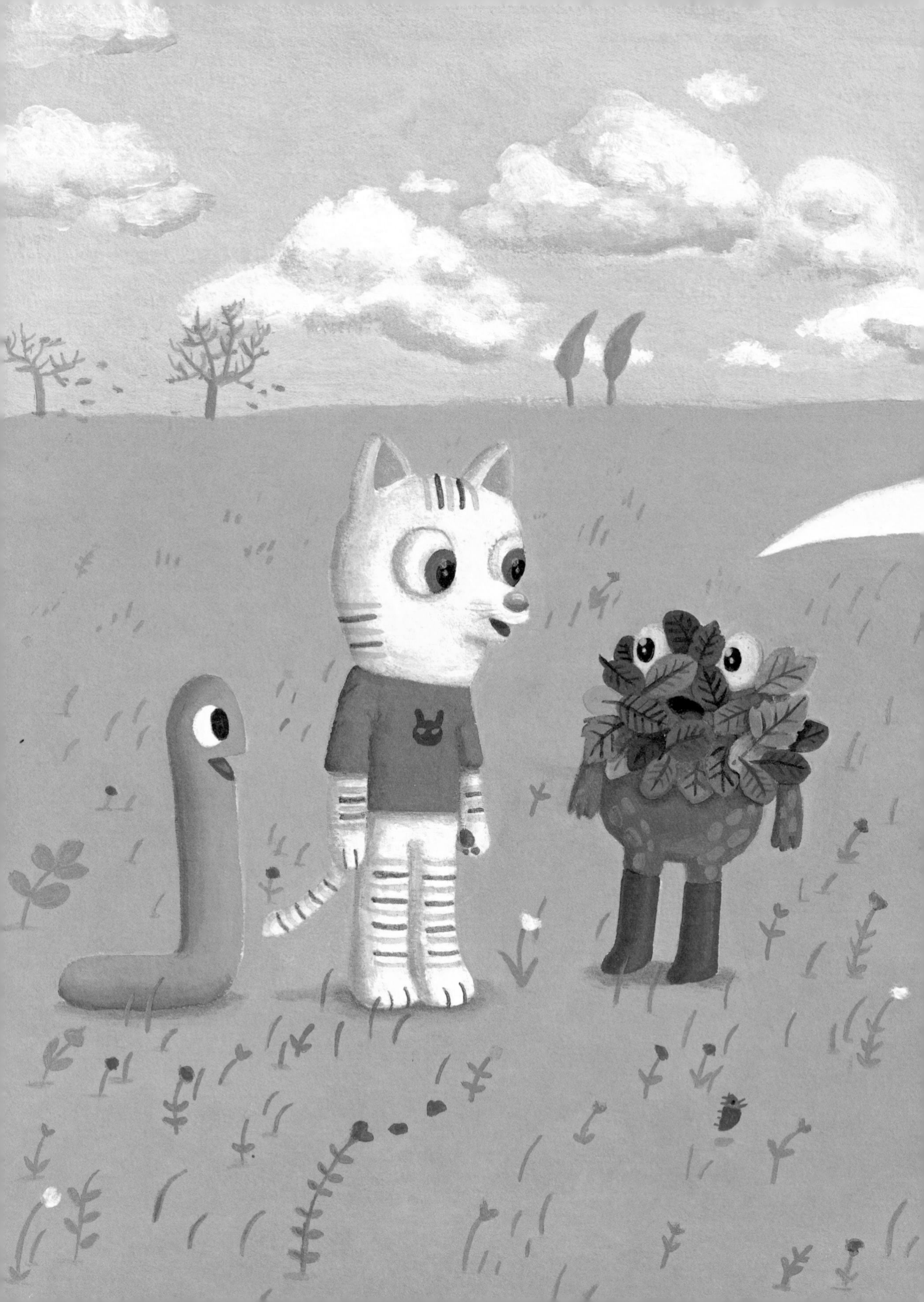

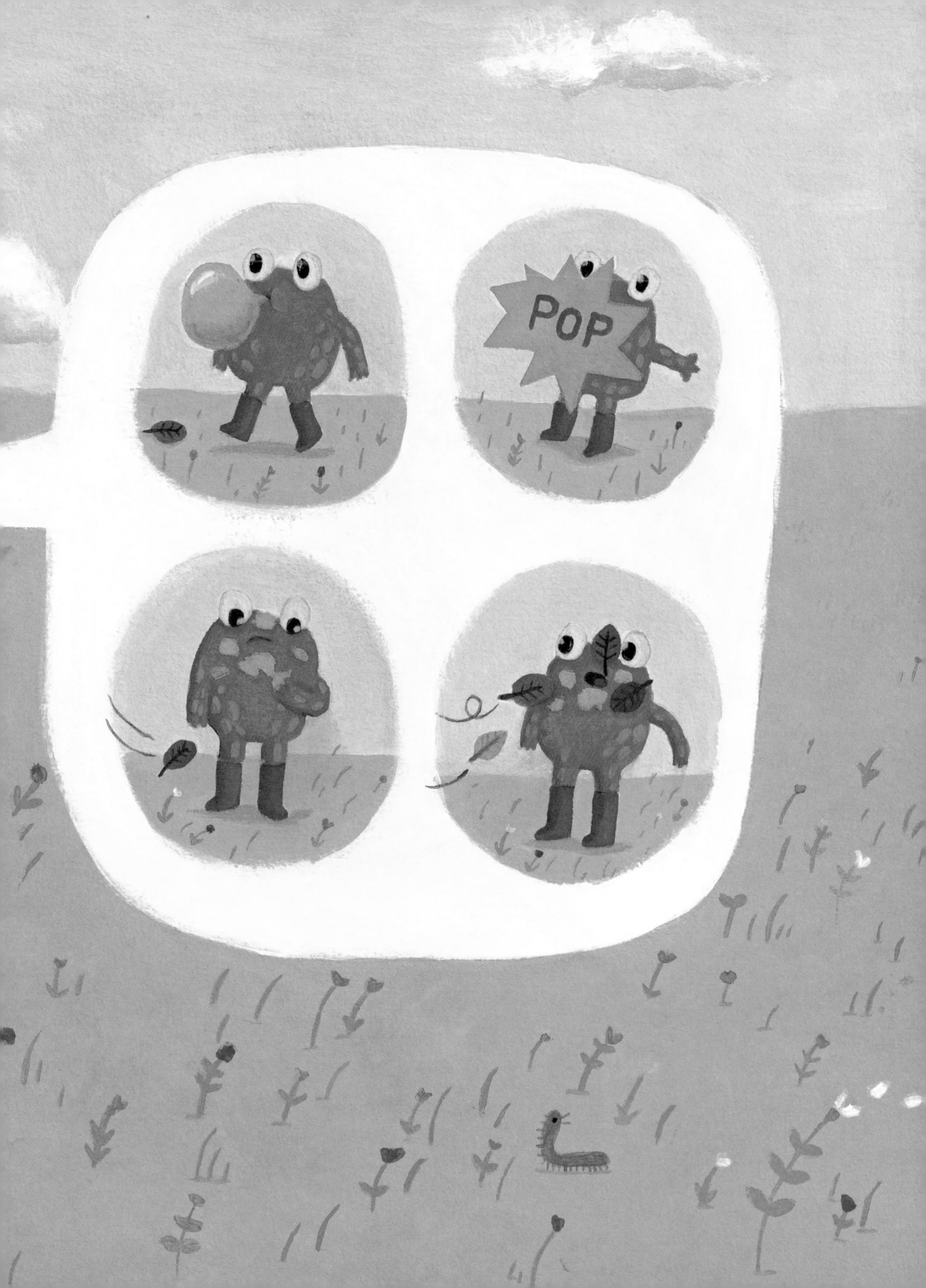
POP

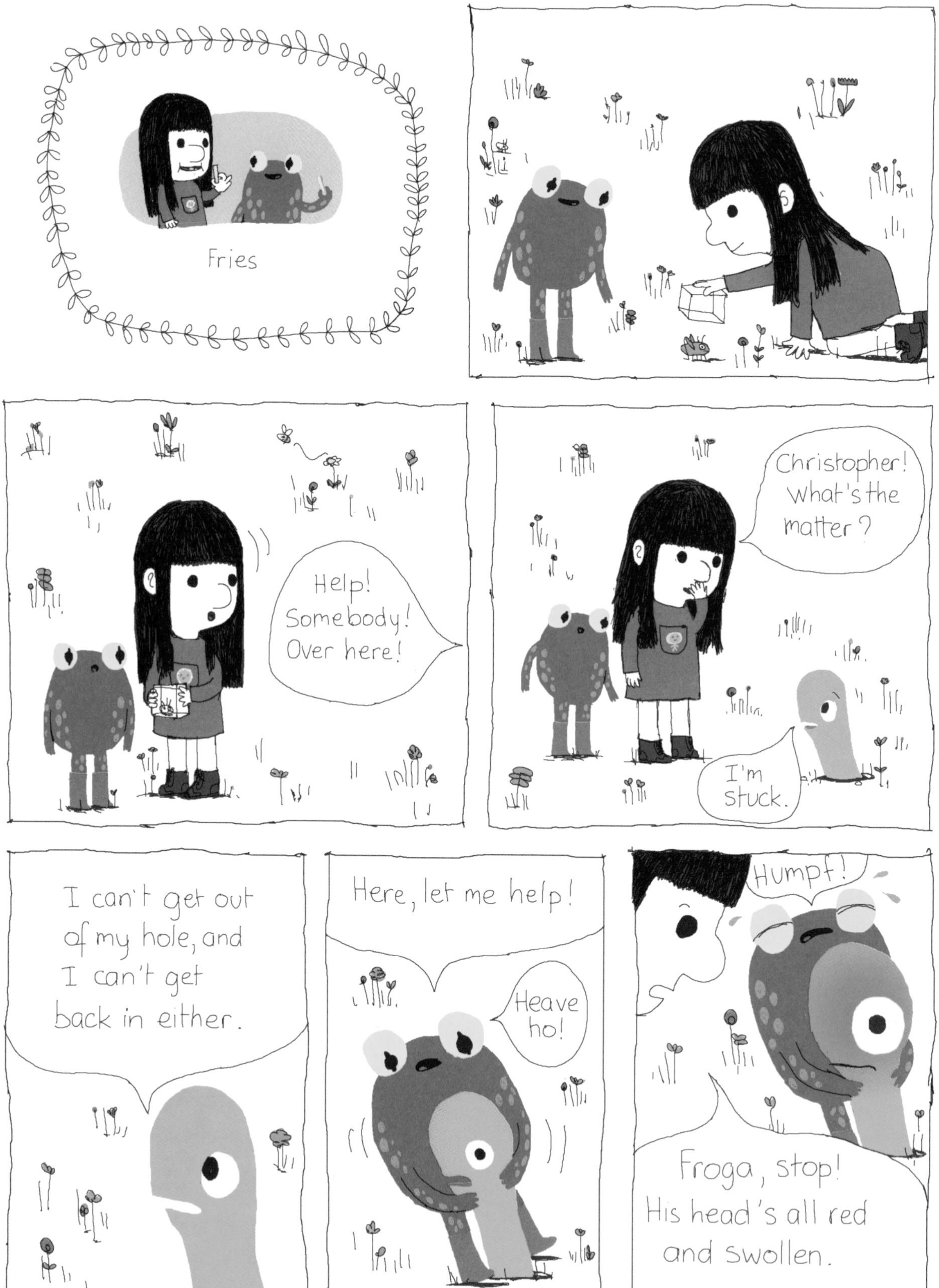
Fries
Help! Somebody! Over here!
Christopher! What's the matter?
I'm stuck.
I can't get out of my hole, and I can't get back in either.
Here, let me help!
Heave ho!
Humpf!
Froga, stop! His head's all red and swollen.

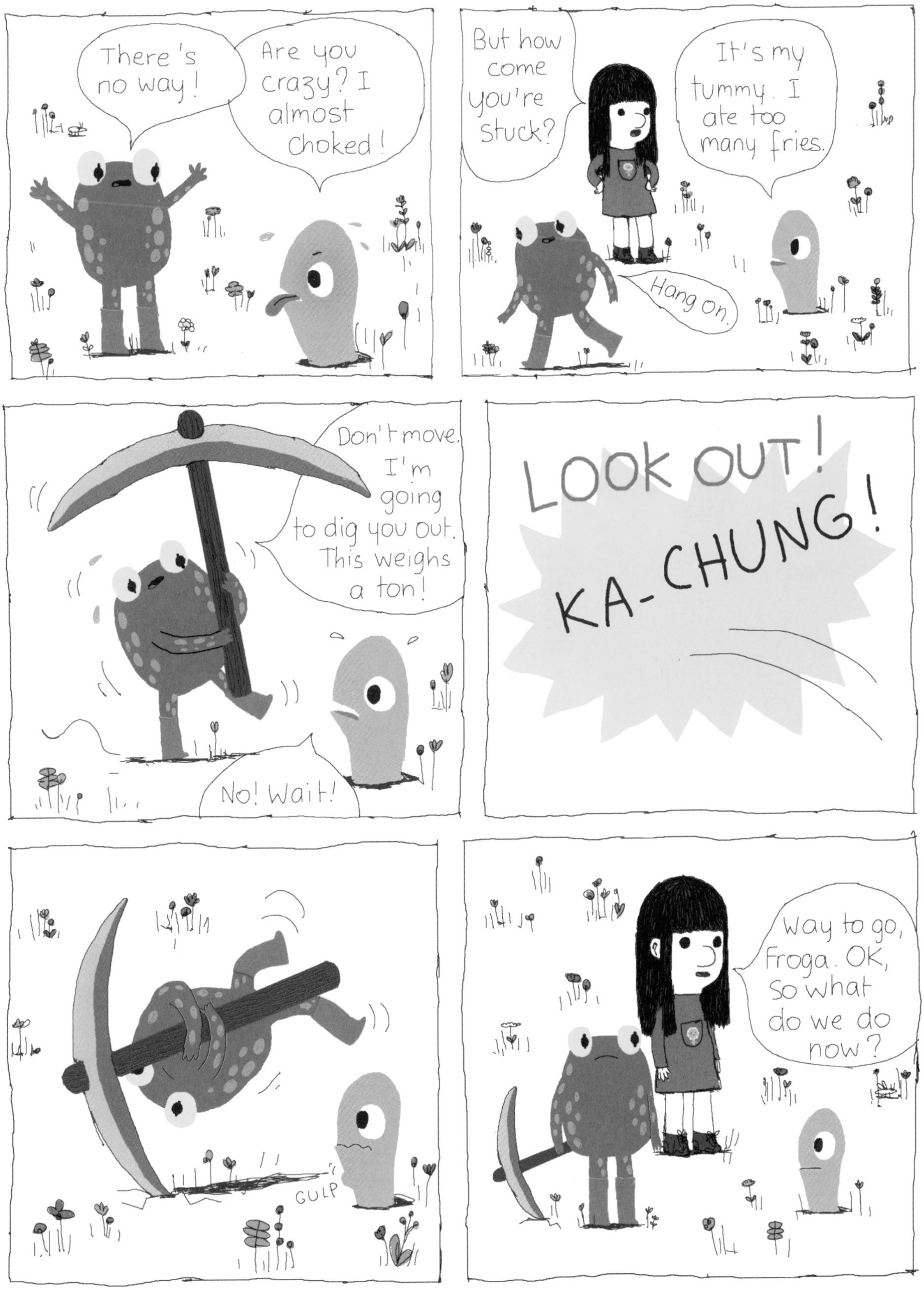
There's no way!
Are you crazy? I almost choked!
But how come you're stuck?
It's my tummy. I ate too many fries.
Hang on.
Don't move. I'm going to dig you out. This weighs a ton!
No! Wait!
LOOK OUT!
KA-CHUNG!
GULP
Way to go, Froga. OK, so what do we do now?

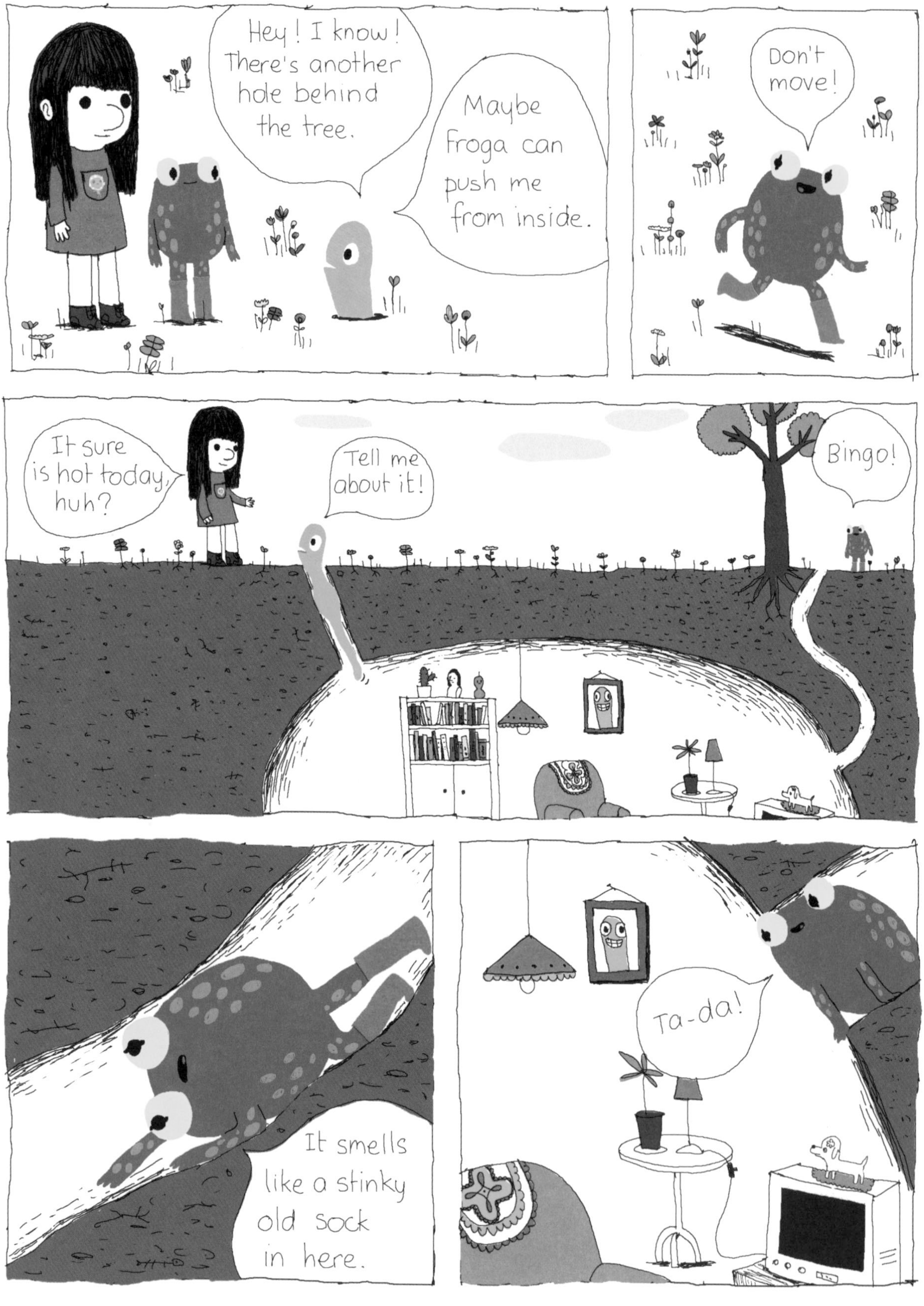
Hey! I know! There's another hole behind the tree.
Maybe Froga can push me from inside.
Don't move!
It sure is hot today, huh?
Tell me about it!
Bingo!
It smells like a stinky old sock in here.
Ta-da!

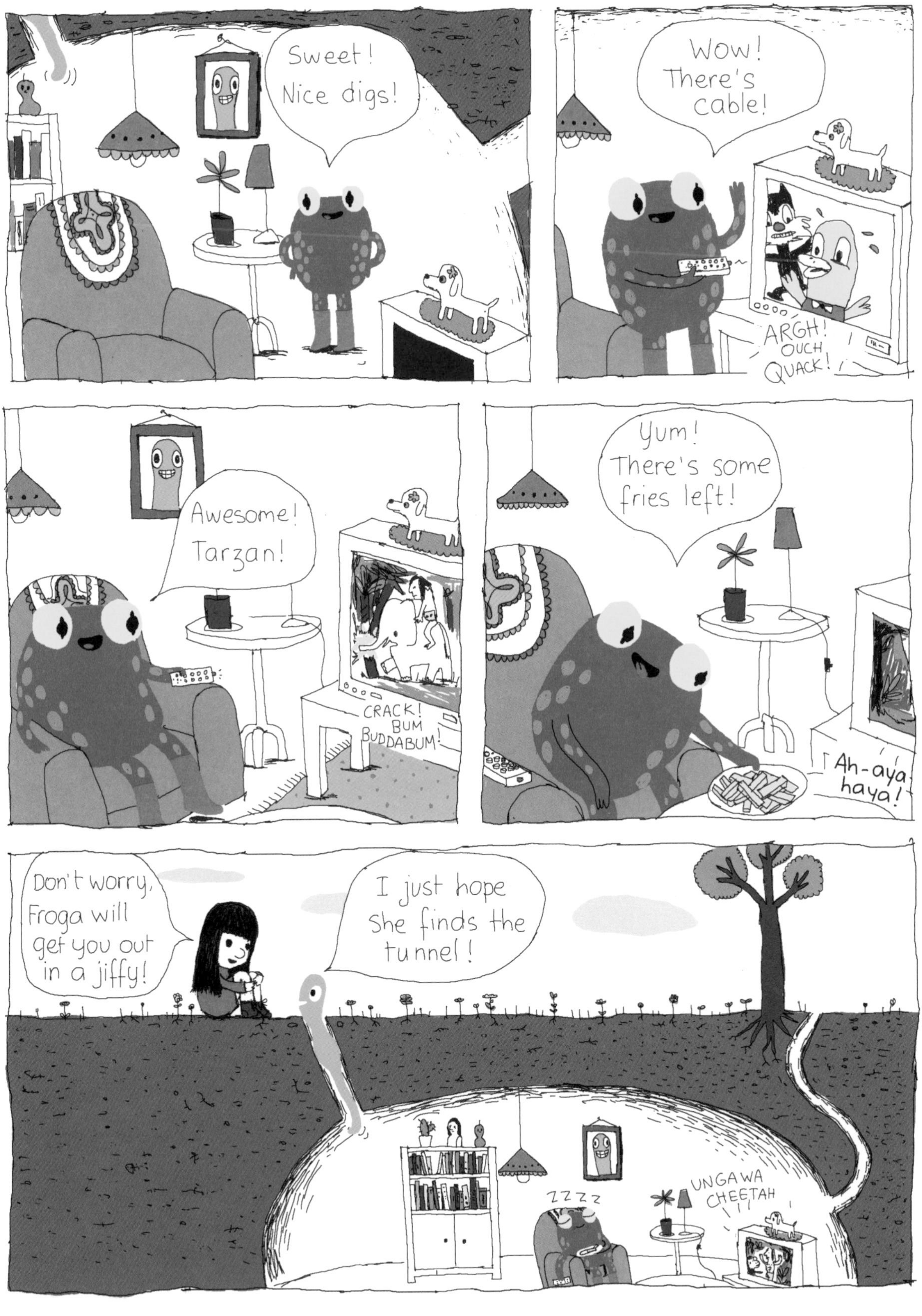
Sweet! Nice digs!
Wow! There's cable!
ARGH! OUCH QUACK!
Awesome! Tarzan!
CRACK! BUM BUDDABUM!
Yum! There's some fries left!
Ah-aya haya!
Don't worry, Froga will get you out in a jiffy!
I just hope she finds the tunnel!
ZZZZ
UNGAWA CHEETAH

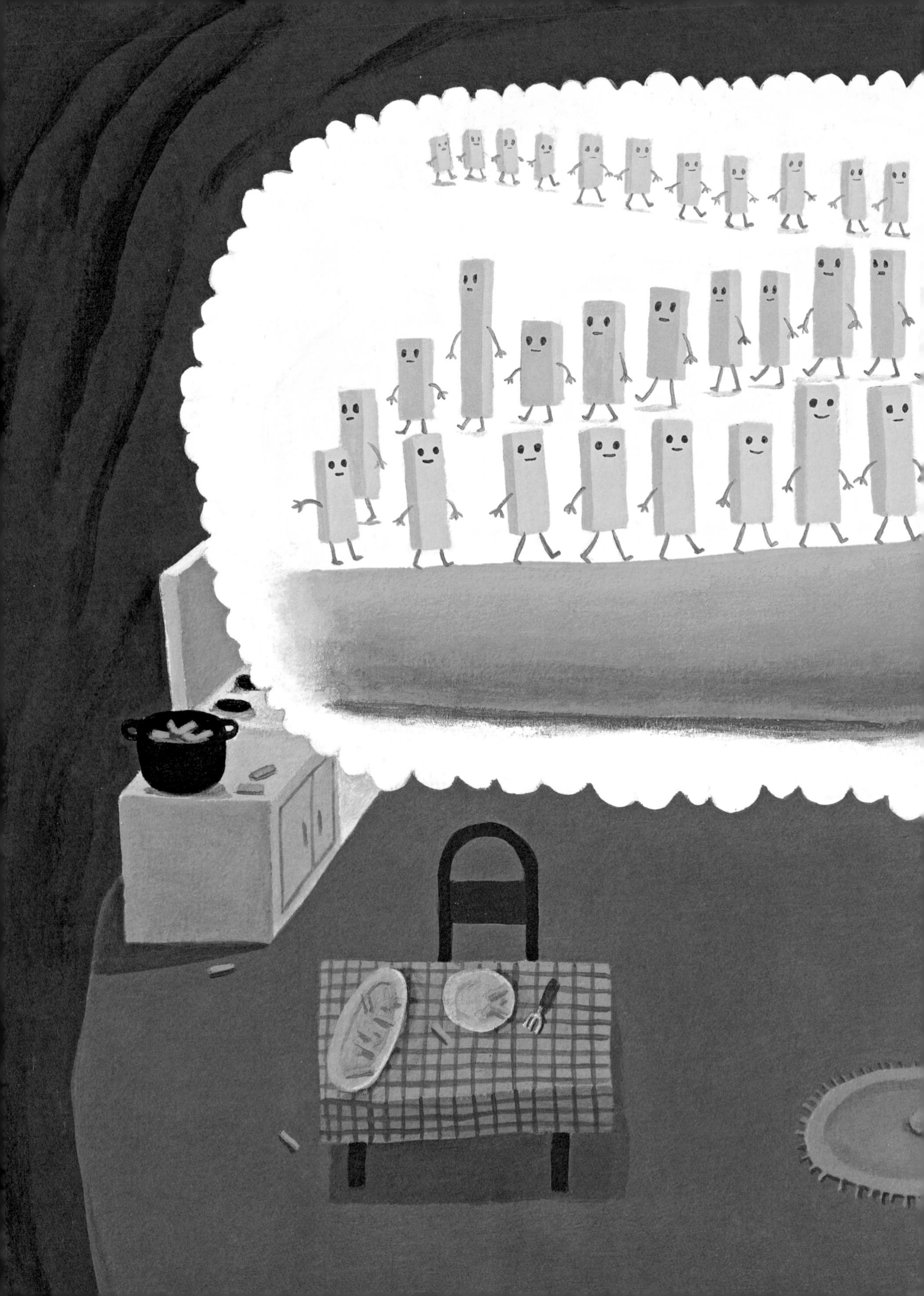

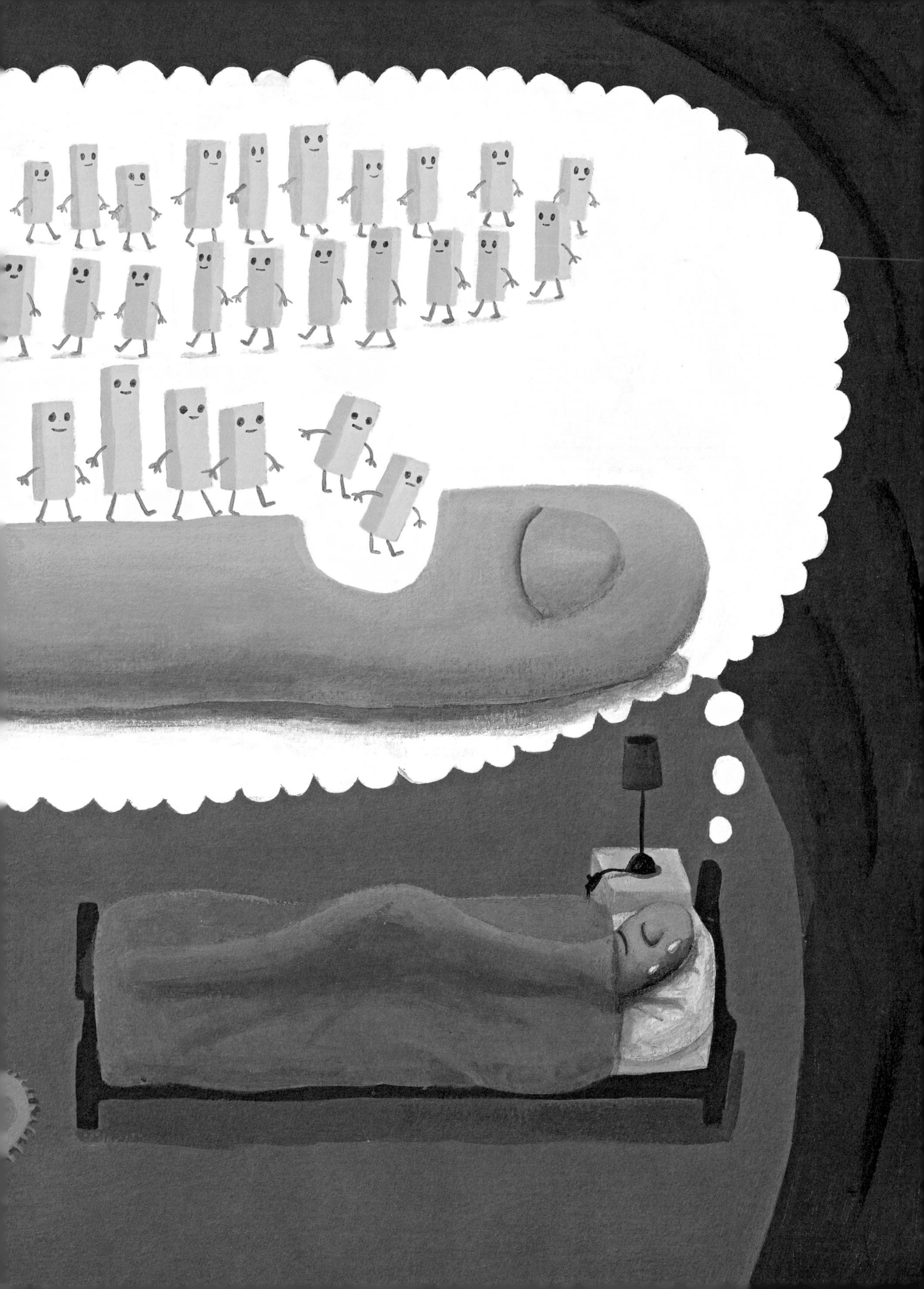

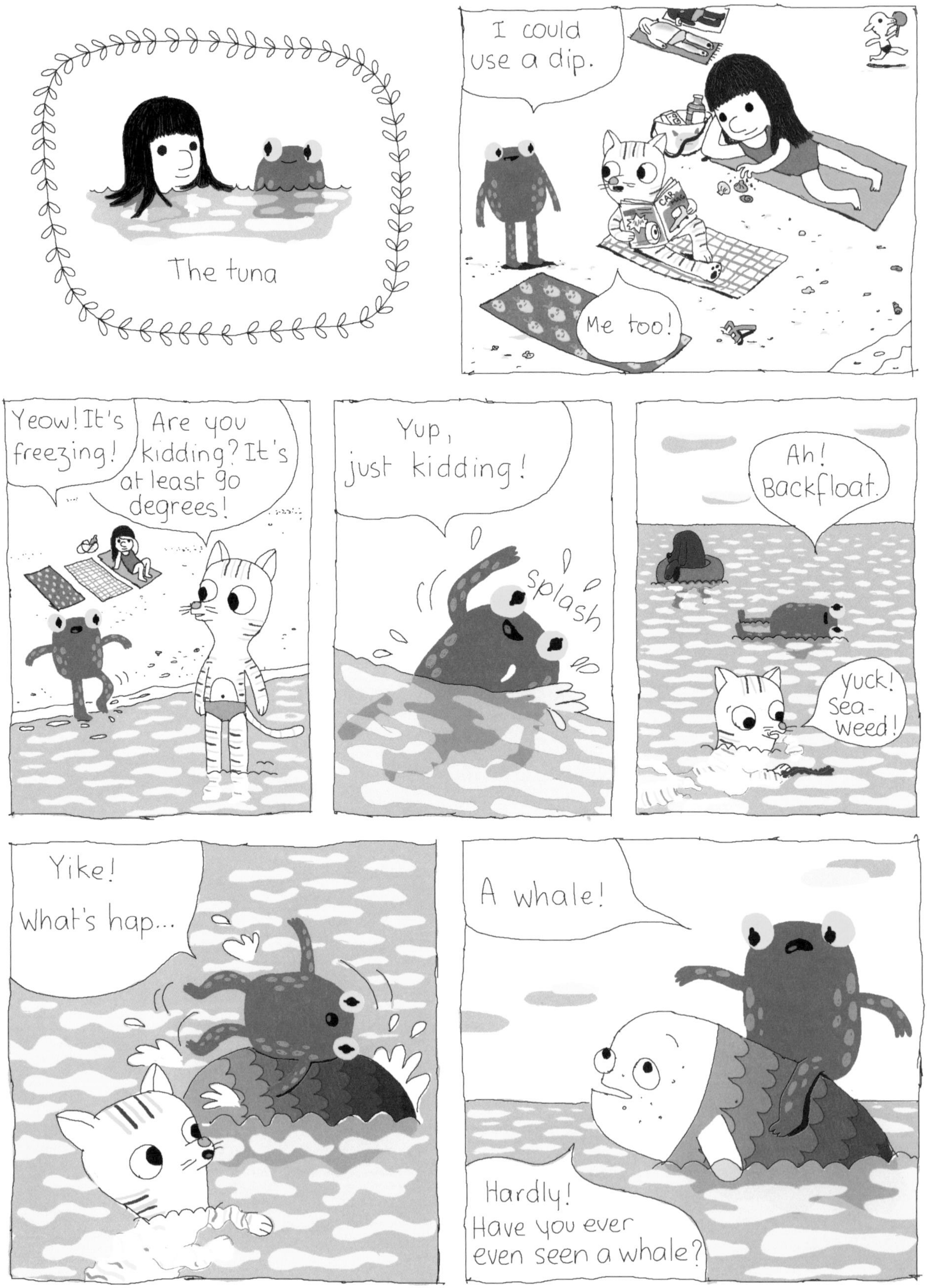
The tuna
I could use a dip.
Me too!
Yeow! It's freezing!
Are you kidding? It's at least 90 degrees!
Yup, just kidding!
Splash
Ah! Backfloat.
Yuck! Sea-weed!
Yike! What's hap...
A whale!
Hardly! Have you ever even seen a whale?

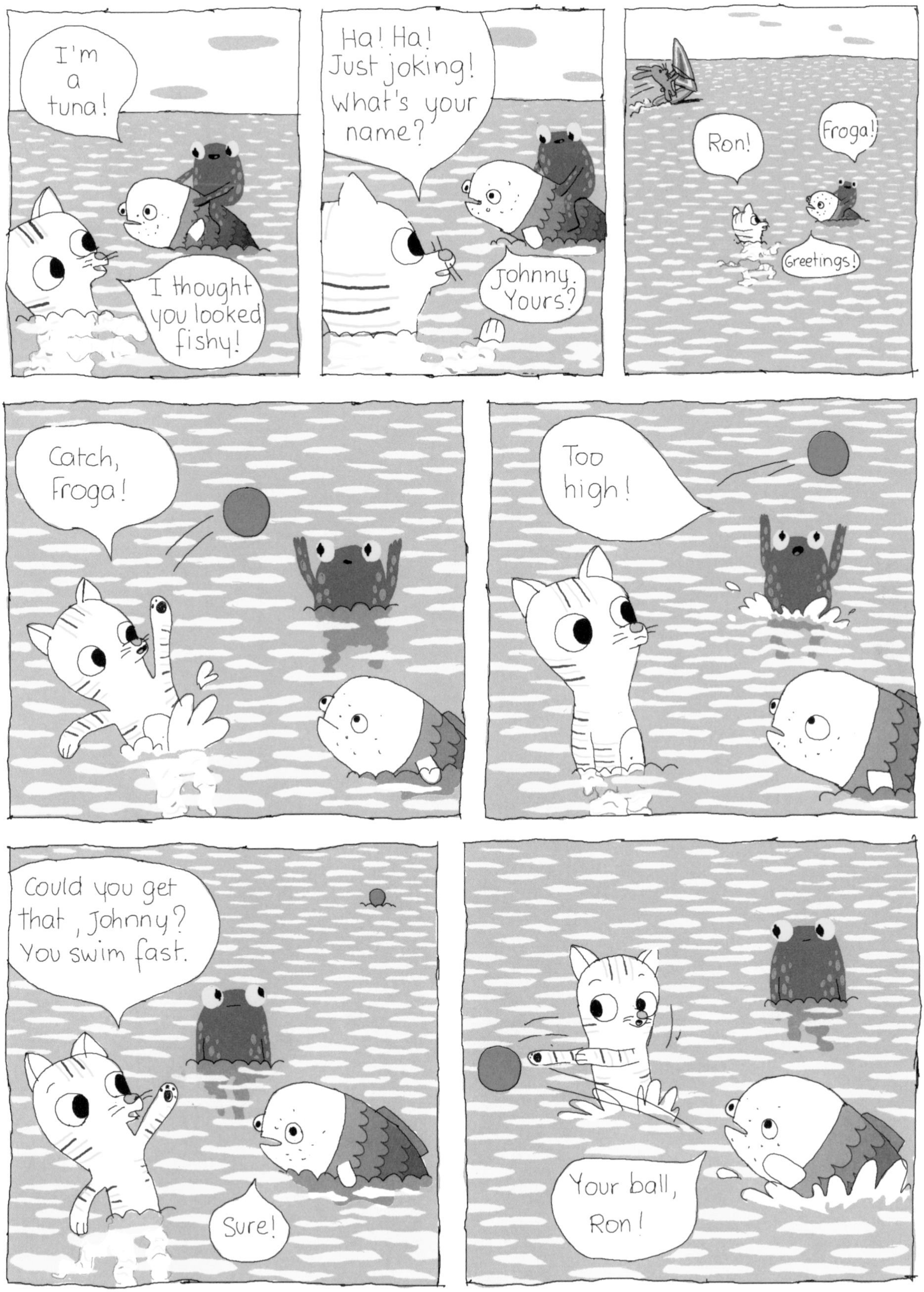
I'm a tuna!
I thought you looked fishy!
Ha! Ha! Just joking! What's your name?
Johnny. Yours?
Ron!
Froga!
Greetings!
Catch, Froga!
Too high!
Could you get that, Johnny? You swim fast.
Sure!
Your ball, Ron!

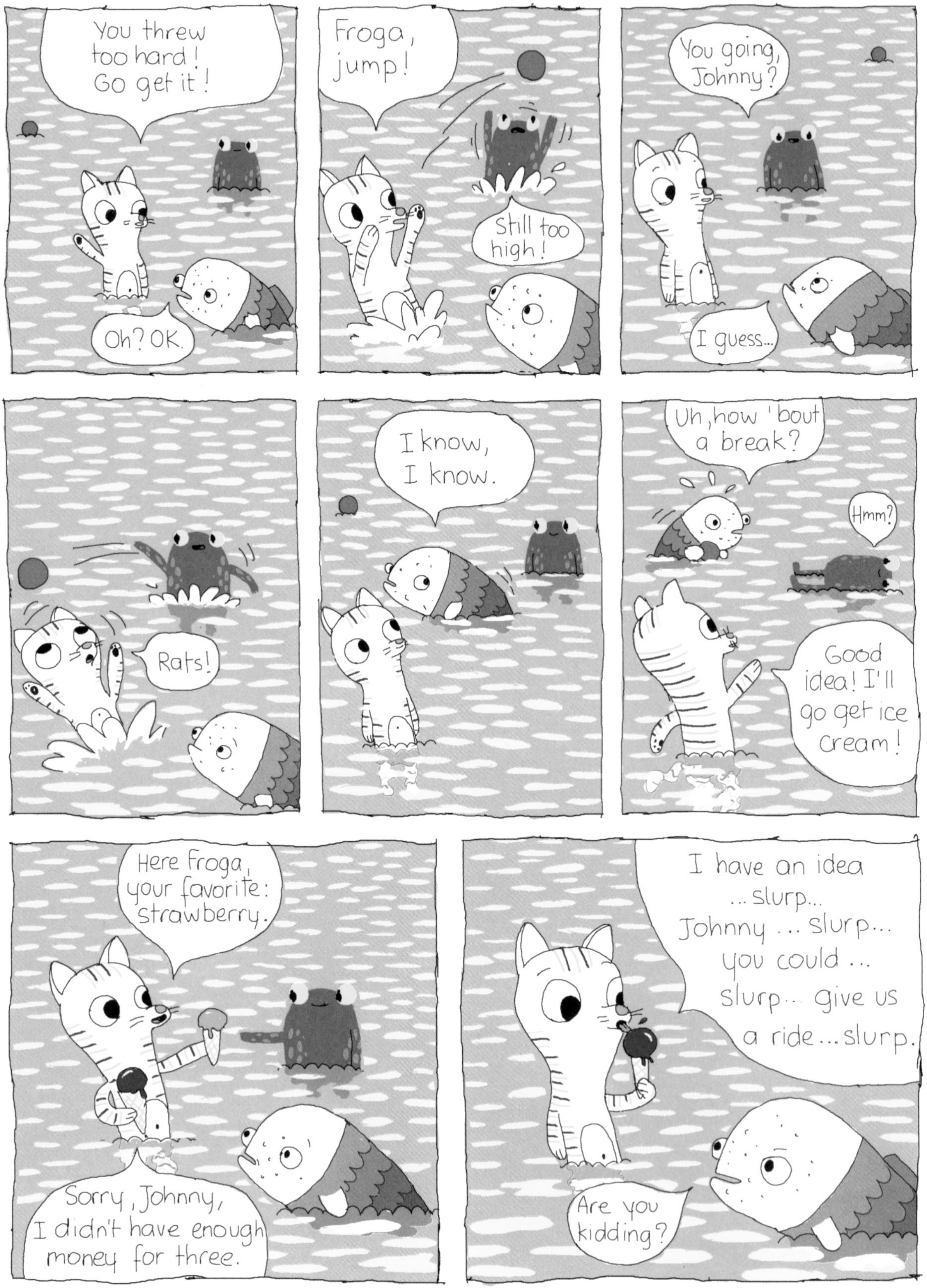

You threw too hard! Go get it!
Oh? OK.
Froga, jump!
Still too high!
You going, Johnny?
I guess...
Rats!
I know, I know.
Uh, how 'bout a break?
Hmm?
Good idea! I'll go get ice cream!
Here Froga, your favorite: strawberry.
Sorry, Johnny, I didn't have enough money for three.
I have an idea ...slurp... Johnny ...slurp... you could ... slurp... give us a ride...slurp.
Are you kidding?

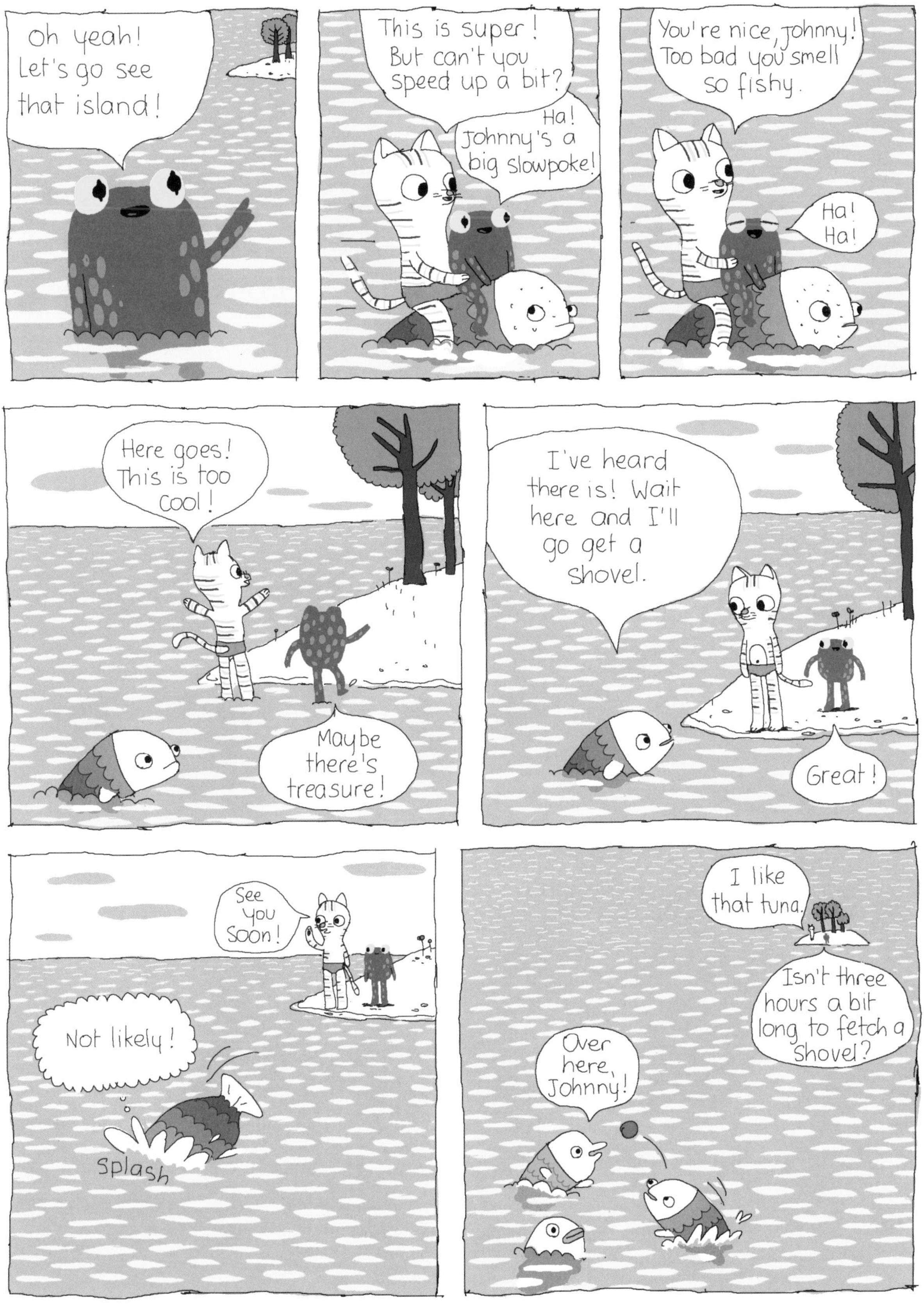
Oh yeah! Let's go see that island!
This is super! But can't you speed up a bit?
Ha! Johnny's a big slowpoke!
You're nice, Johnny! Too bad you smell so fishy.
Ha! Ha!
Here goes! This is too cool!
Maybe there's treasure!
I've heard there is! Wait here and I'll go get a shovel.
Great!
See you soon!
Not likely!
Splash
I like that tuna.
Isn't three hours a bit long to fetch a shovel?
Over here, Johnny!

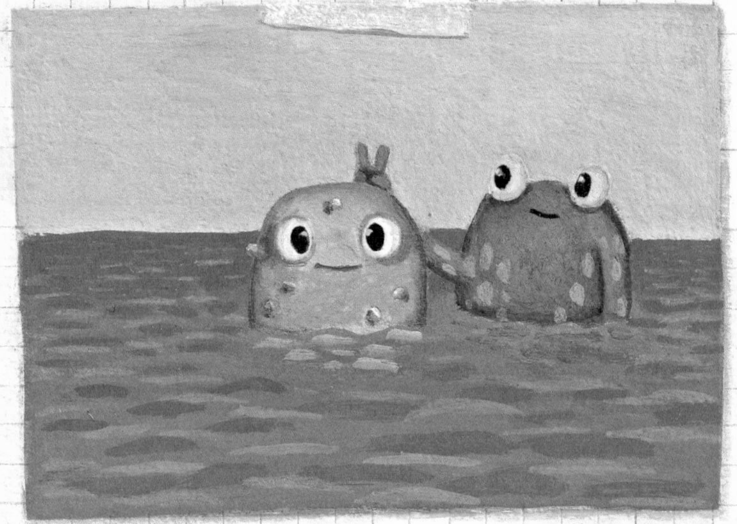

← Froga and Johnny

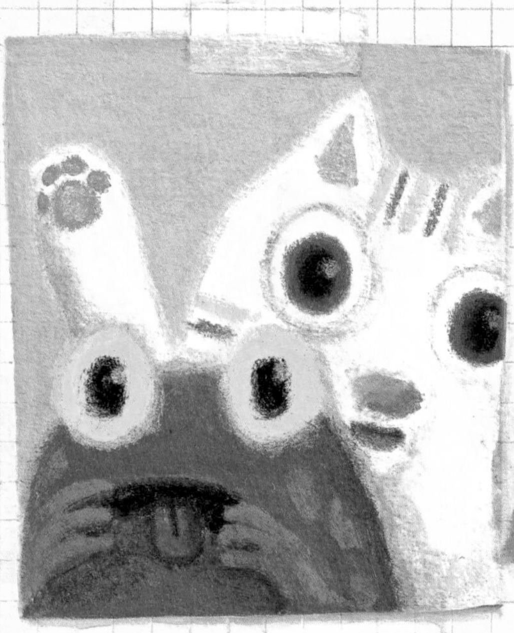

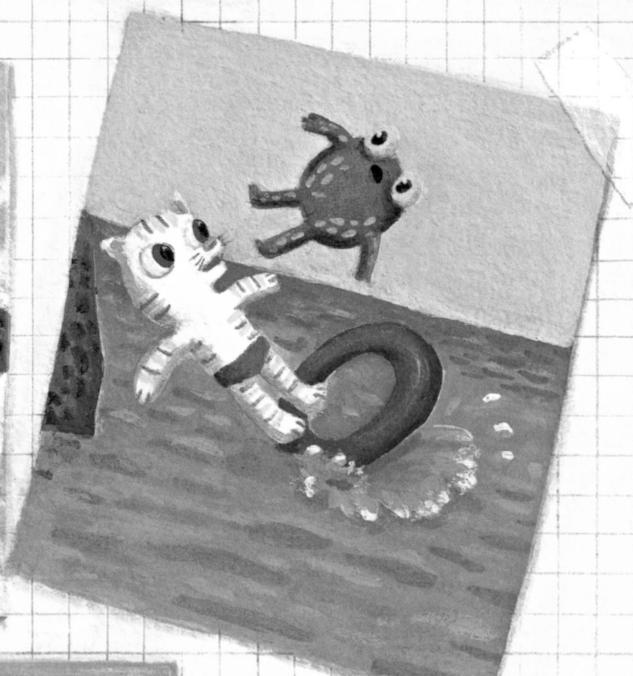

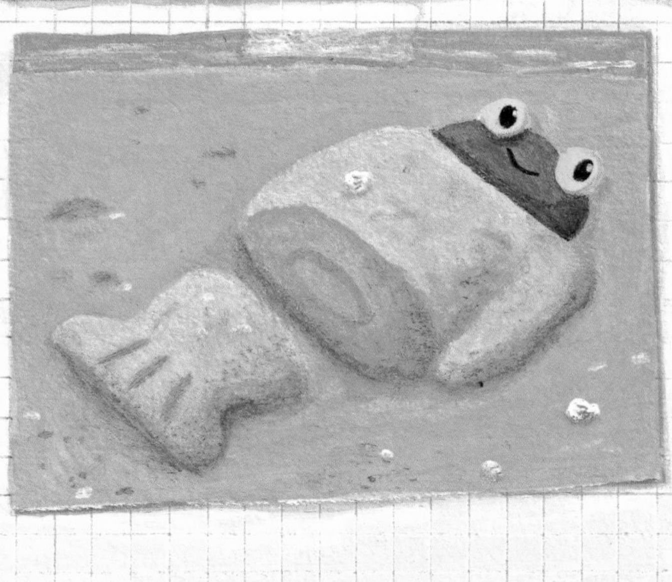

← Froga the tuna

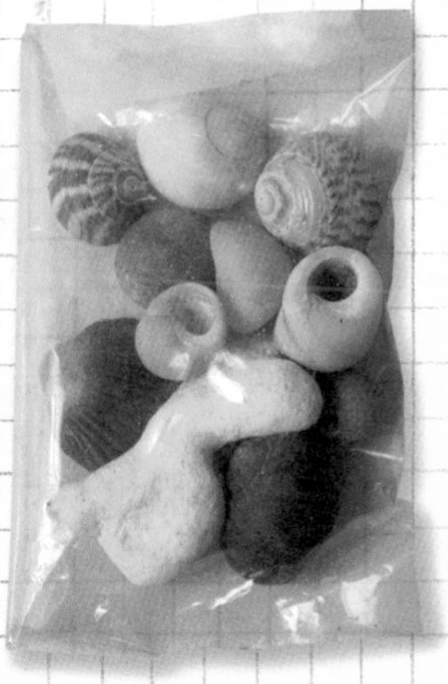

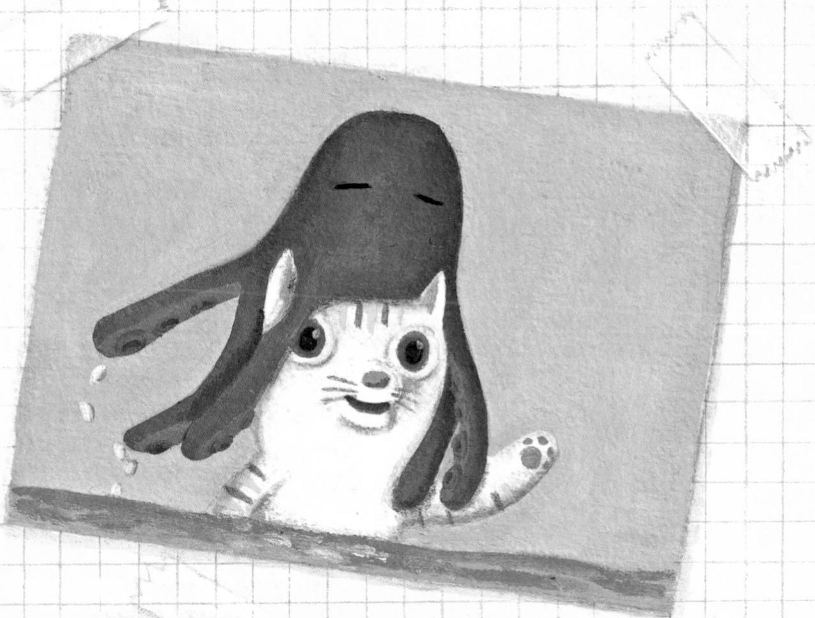

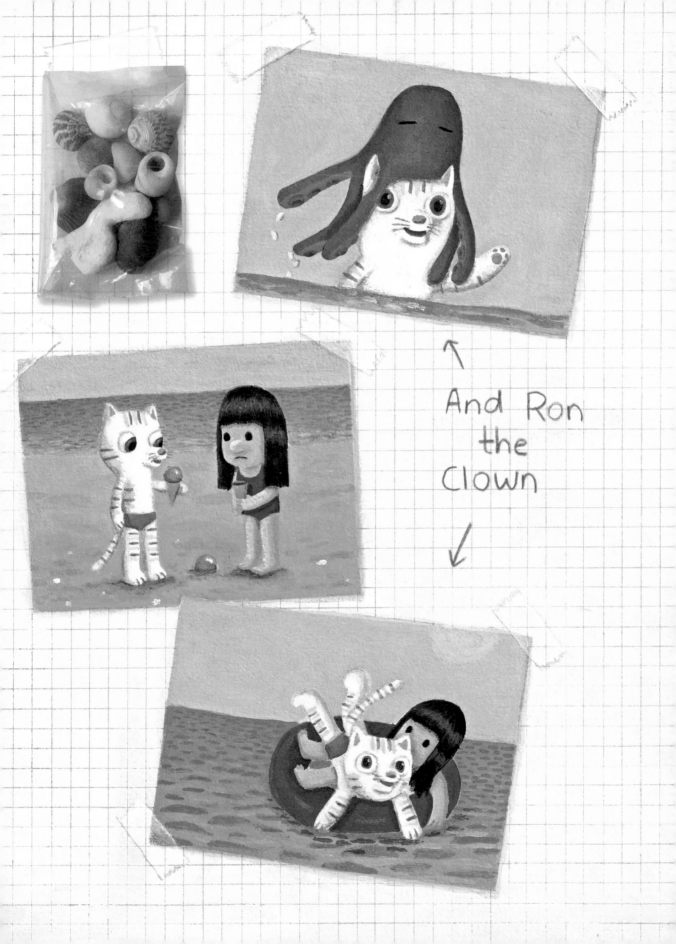

And Ron the Clown

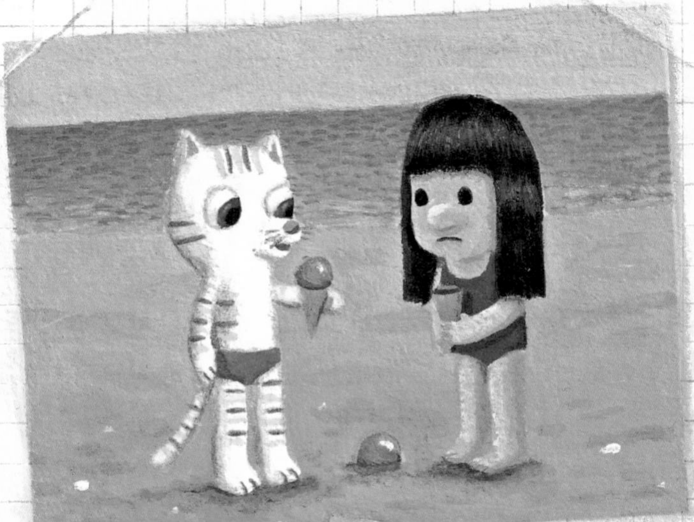

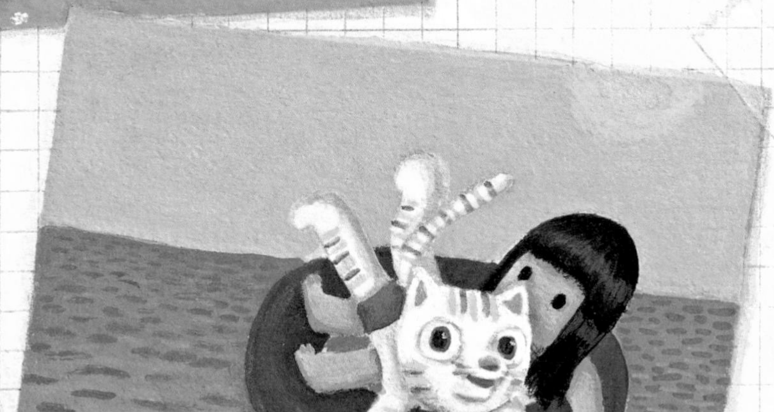

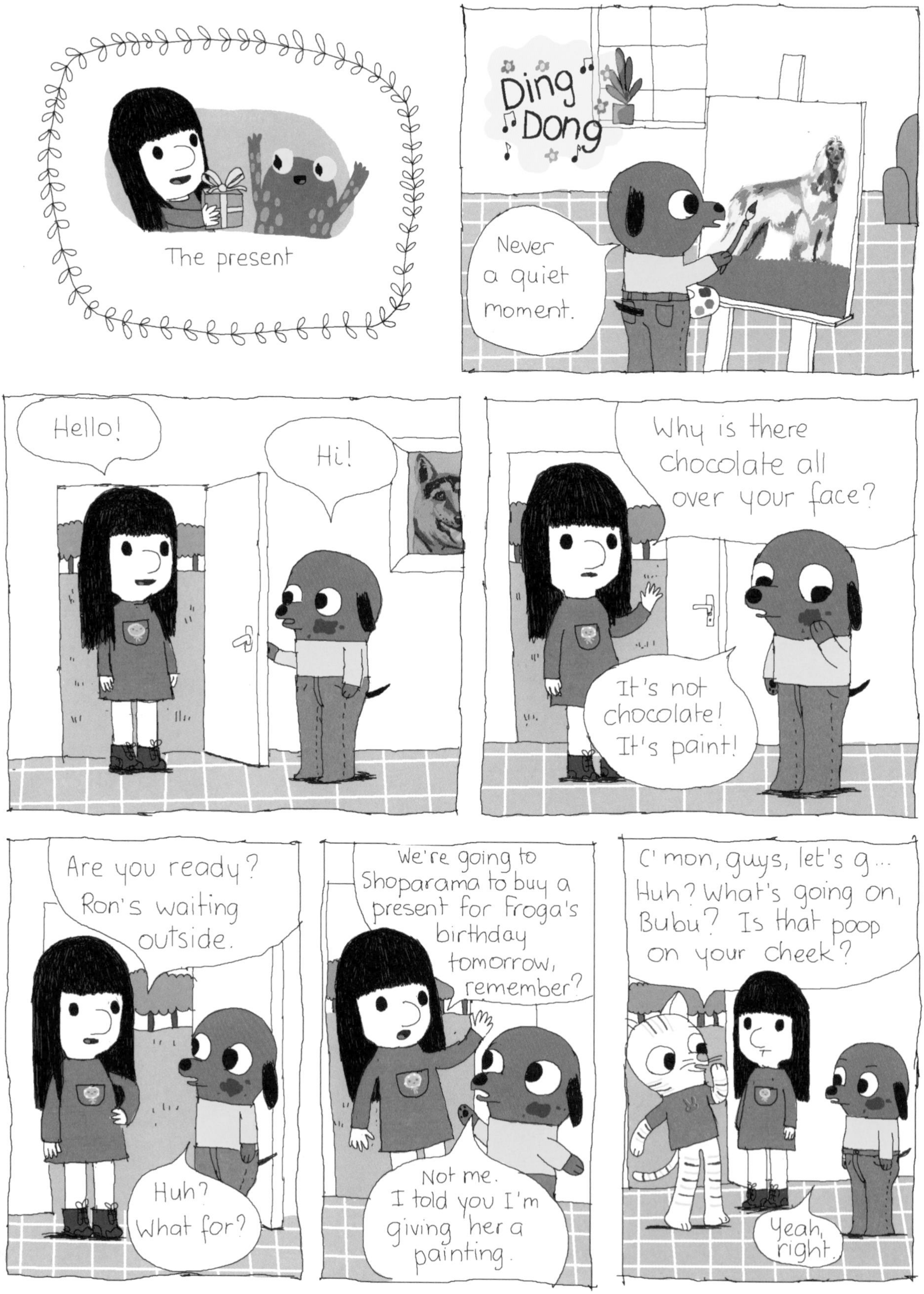
The present
Ding Dong
Never a quiet moment.
Hello!
Hi!
Why is there chocolate all over your face?
It's not chocolate! It's paint!
Are you ready? Ron's waiting outside.
Huh? What for?
We're going to Shoparama to buy a present for Froga's birthday tomorrow, remember?
Not me. I told you I'm giving her a painting.
C'mon, guys, let's g... Huh? What's going on, Bubu? Is that poop on your cheek?
Yeah, right.

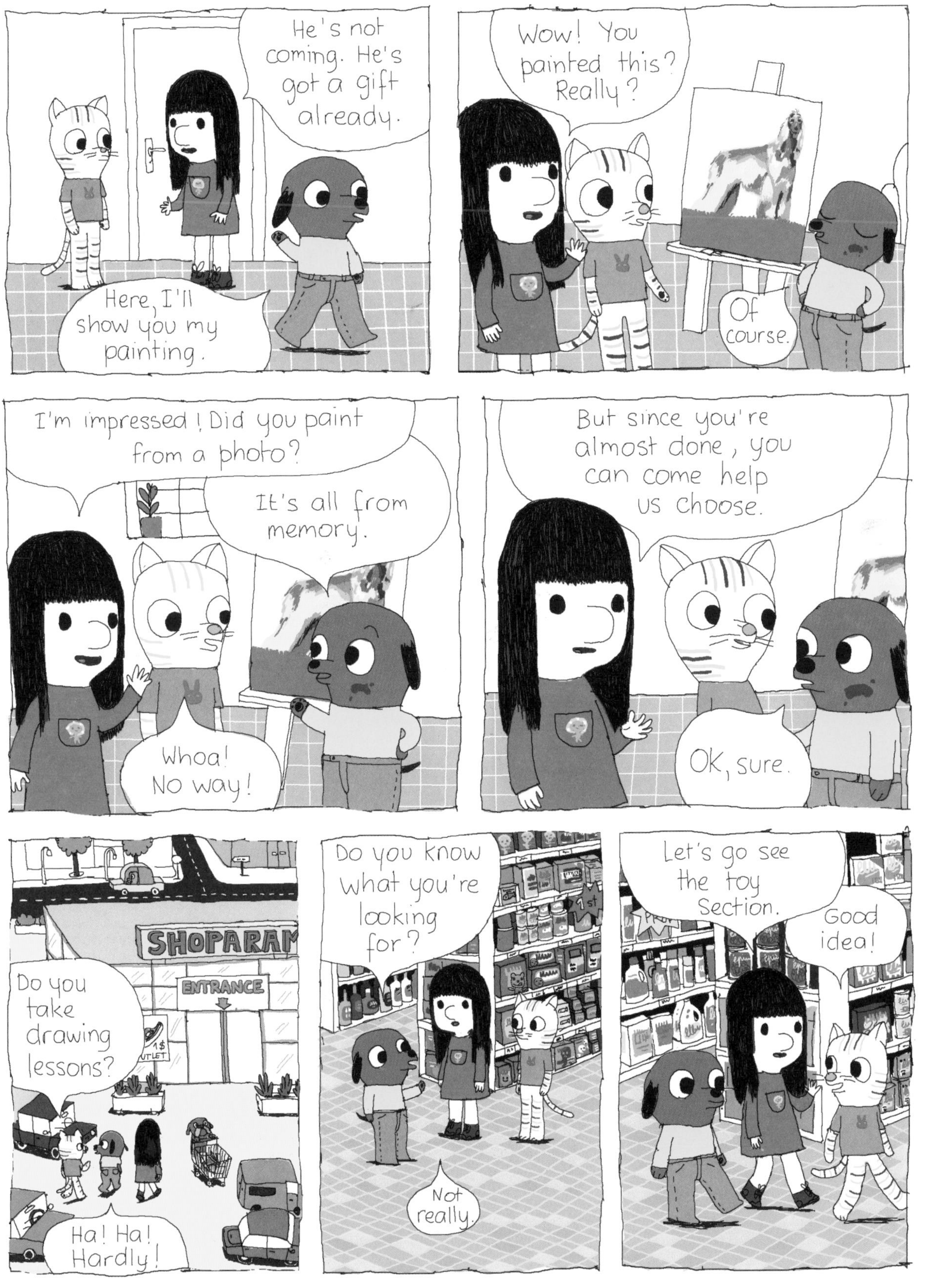
He's not coming. He's got a gift already.
Here, I'll show you my painting.
Wow! You painted this? Really?
Of course.
I'm impressed! Did you paint from a photo?
It's all from memory.
Whoa! No way!
But since you're almost done, you can come help us choose.
Ok, sure.
SHOPARAMA
ENTRANCE
Do you take drawing lessons?
Ha! Ha! Hardly!
Do you know what you're looking for?
Not really.
Let's go see the toy section.
Good idea!

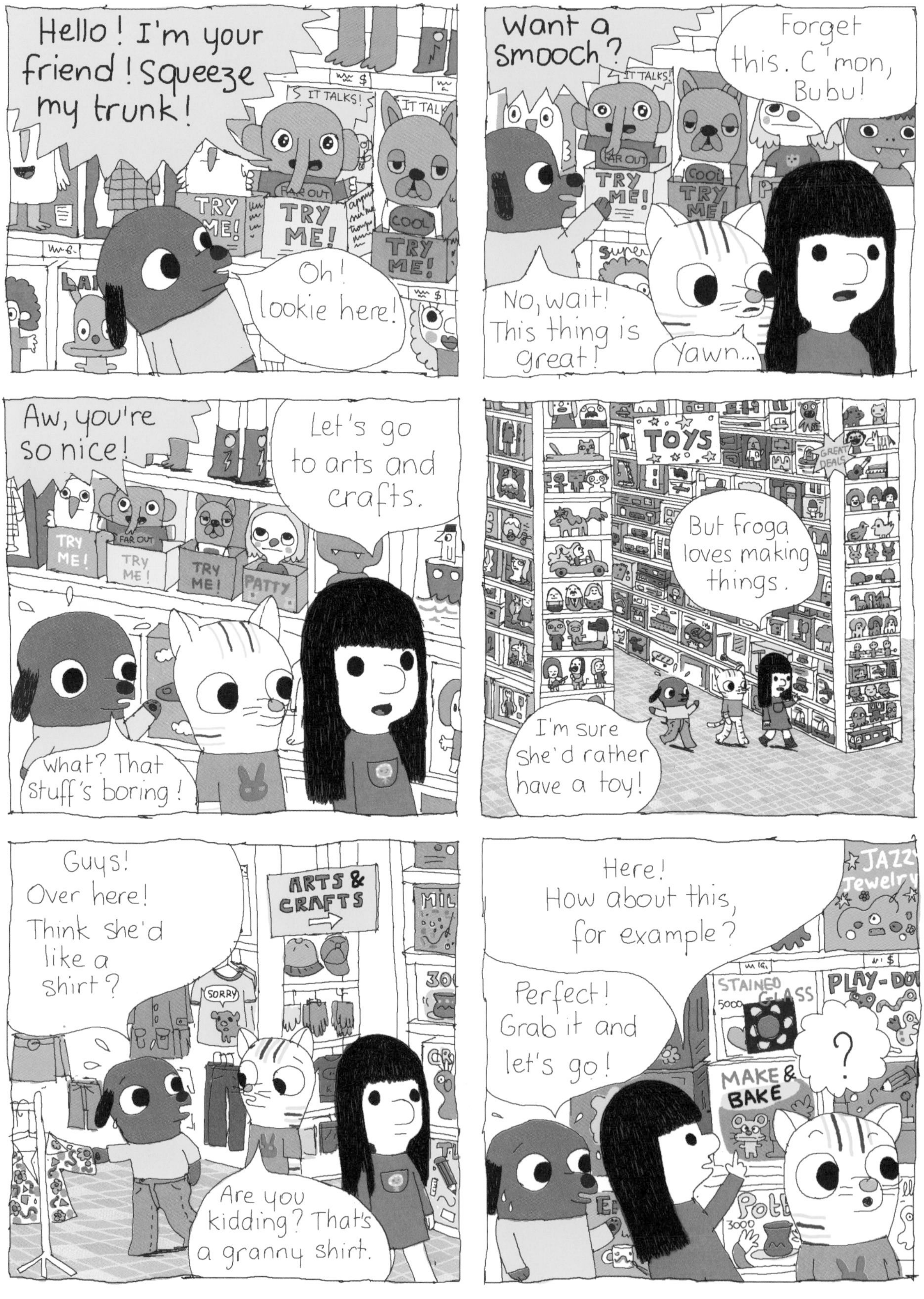
Hello! I'm your friend! Squeeze my trunk!
IT TALKS!
IT TALKS!
FAR OUT
TRY ME!
TRY ME!
COOL
TRY ME!
Oh! lookie here!
Want a smooch?
Forget this. C'mon, Bubu!
IT TALKS!
FAR OUT
TRY ME!
COOL
TRY ME!
No, wait! This thing is great!
Yawn...
Aw, you're so nice!
Let's go to arts and crafts.
TRY ME!
FAR OUT
TRY ME!
TRY ME!
PATTY
What? That stuff's boring!
TOYS
GREAT DEALS
But Froga loves making things.
I'm sure she'd rather have a toy!
Guys! Over here! Think she'd like a shirt?
ARTS & CRAFTS
SORRY
Are you kidding? That's a granny shirt.
Here! How about this, for example?
JAZZY Jewelry
STAINED GLASS
5000
PLAY-DO
Perfect! Grab it and let's go!
MAKE & BAKE
?
3000

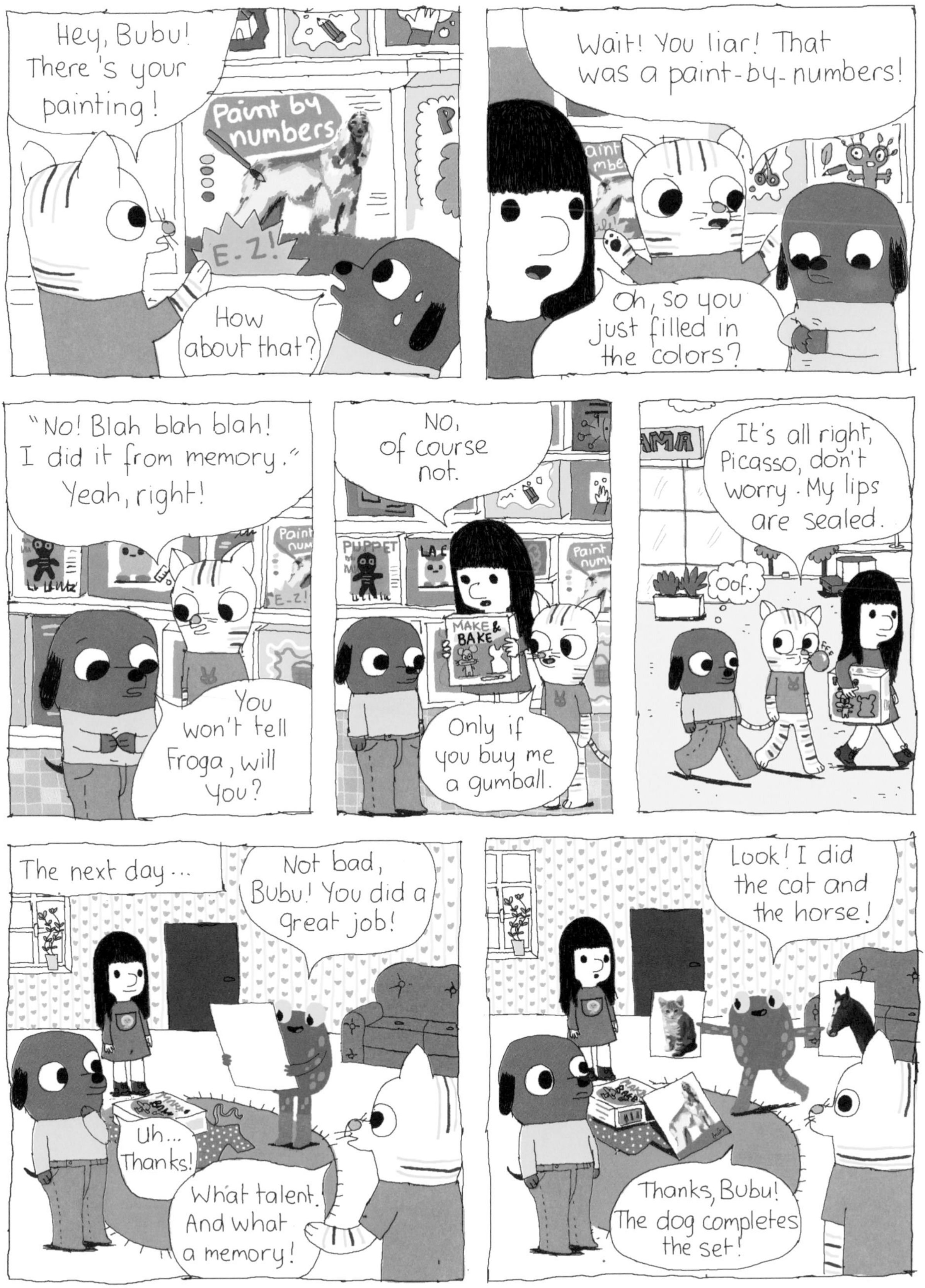
Hey, Bubu! There's your painting!
Paint by numbers
E-Z!
How about that?
Wait! You liar! That was a paint-by-numbers!
Oh, so you just filled in the colors?
"No! Blah blah blah! I did it from memory." Yeah, right!
You won't tell Froga, will you?
No, of course not.
Only if you buy me a gumball.
MAKE & BAKE
It's all right, Picasso, don't worry. My lips are sealed.
Oof.
The next day...
Not bad, Bubu! You did a great job!
Uh... Thanks!
What talent! And what a memory!
Look! I did the cat and the horse!
Thanks, Bubu! The dog completes the set!

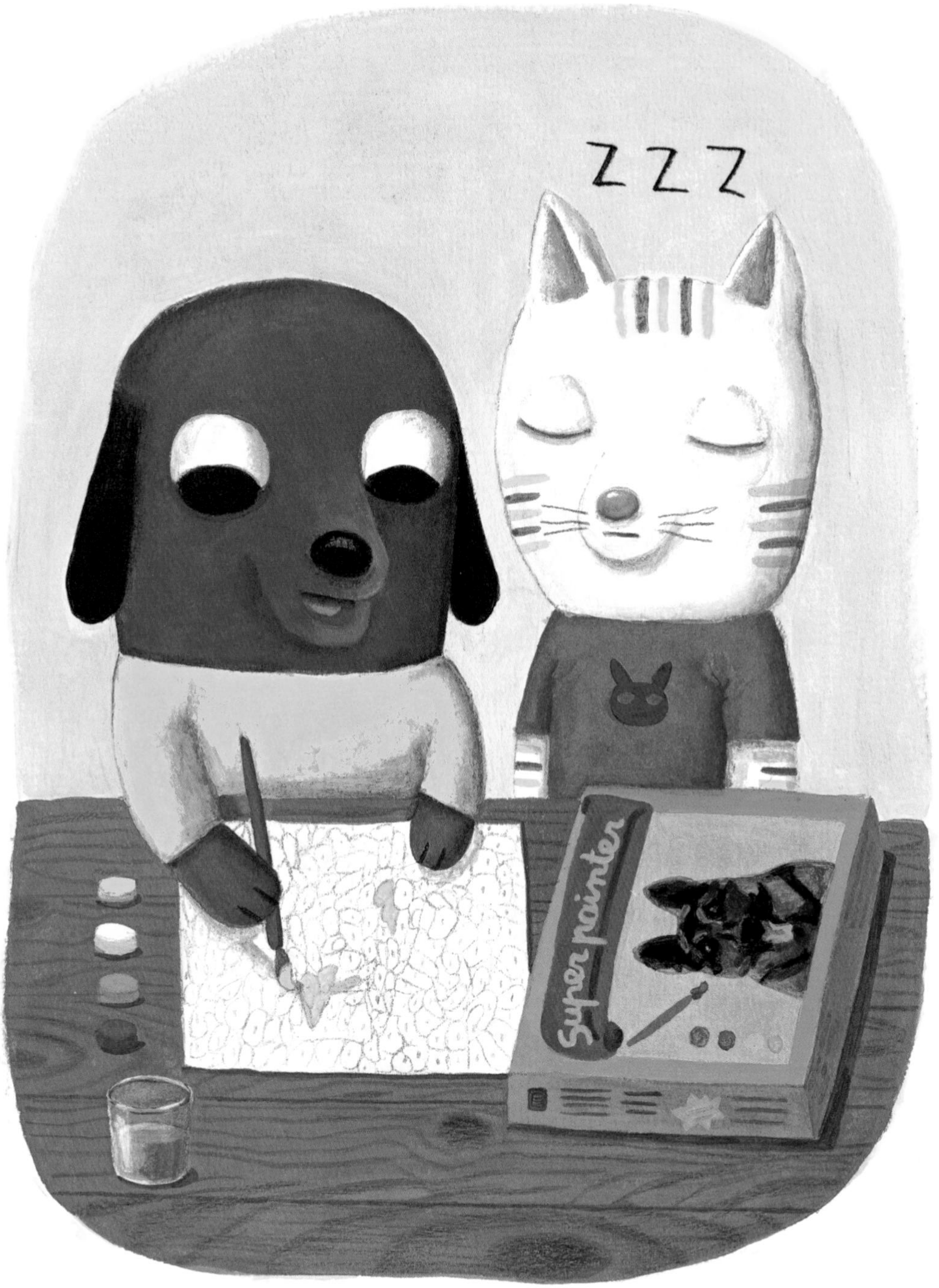
z z z
Super painter

- And after that, you fill in all the number 3 spaces, and then the number 6s, and then...

uh, do you think you got
all the colors right?

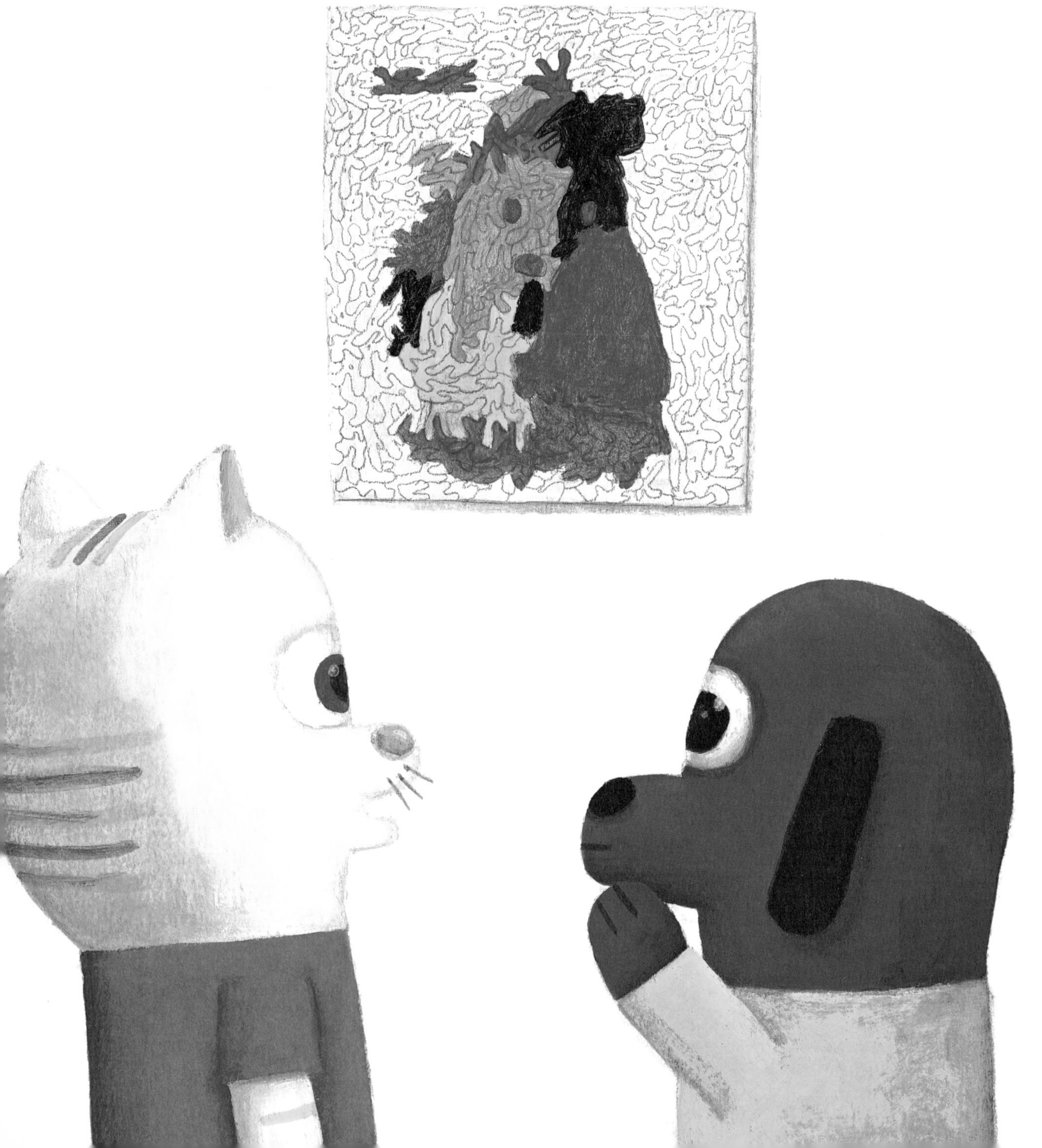

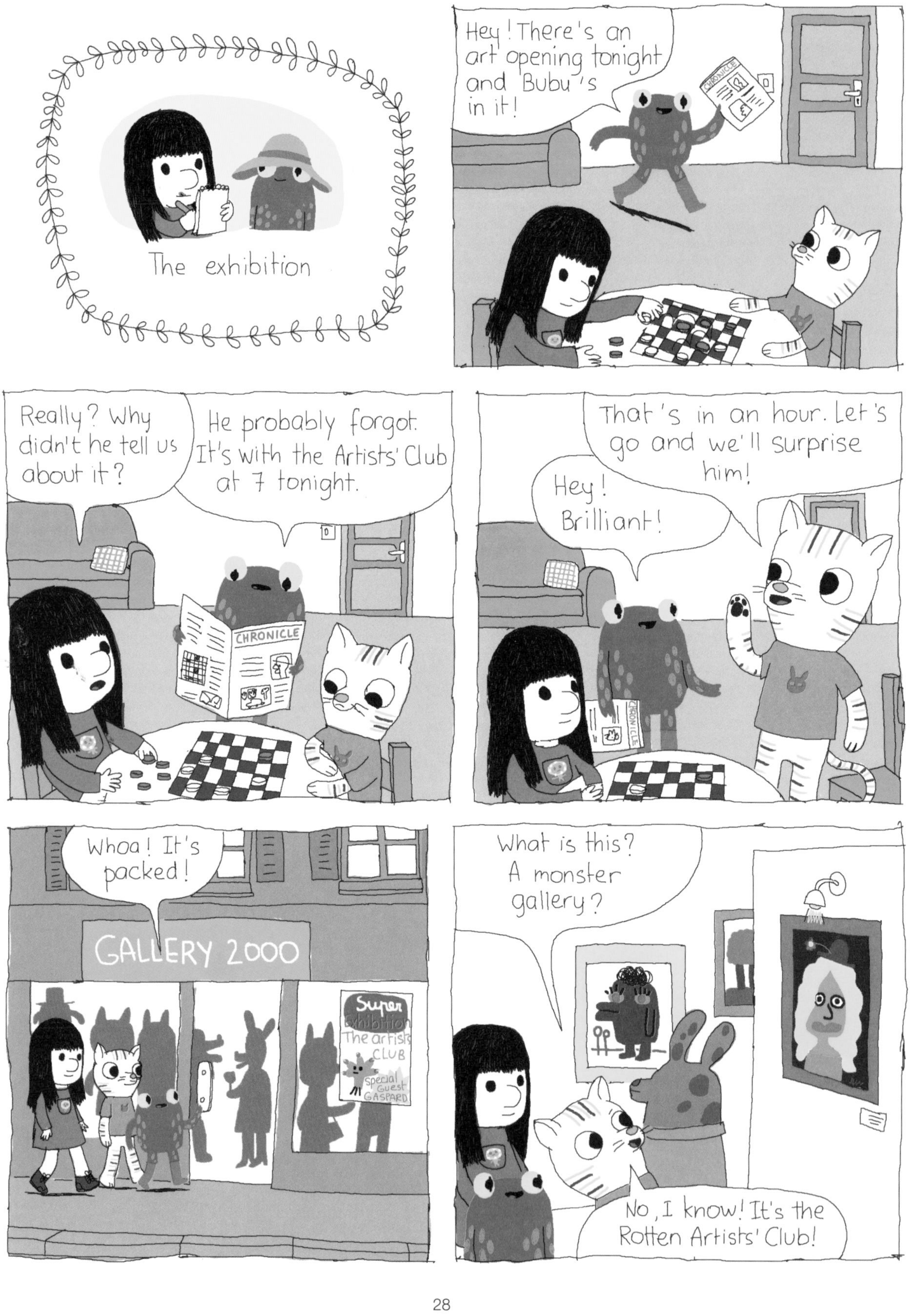
The exhibition
Hey! There's an art opening tonight and Bubu's in it!
CHRONICLE
Really? Why didn't he tell us about it?
He probably forgot. It's with the Artists' Club at 7 tonight.
CHRONICLE
That's in an hour. Let's go and we'll surprise him!
Hey! Brilliant!
CHRONICLE
Whoa! It's packed!
GALLERY 2000
Super exhibition
The artists CLUB
Special Guest GASPARD
What is this? A monster gallery?
No, I know! It's the Rotten Artists' Club!

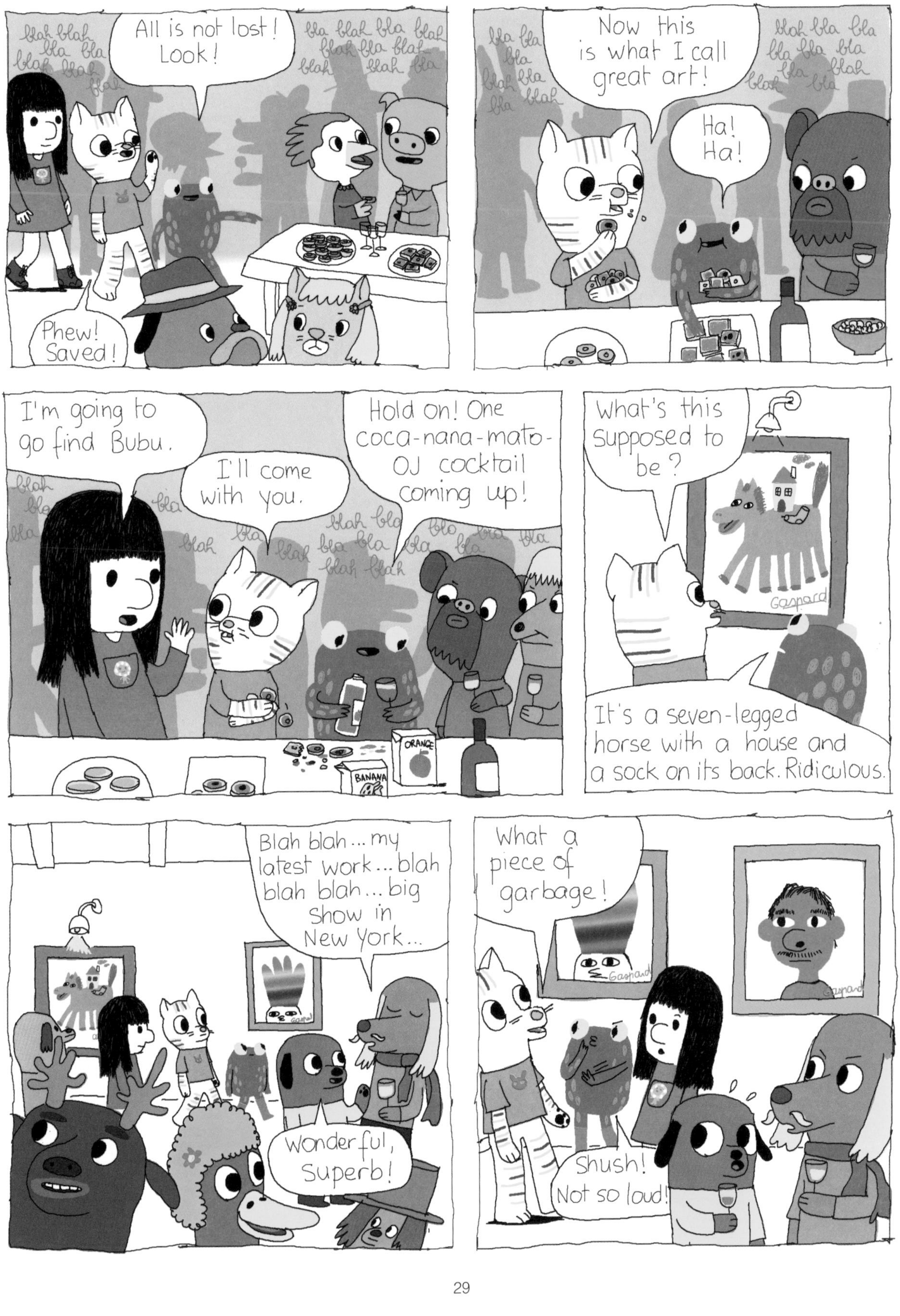
All is not lost! Look!
Phew! Saved!
Now this is what I call great art!
Ha! Ha!
I'm going to go find Bubu.
I'll come with you.
Hold on! One coca-nana-mato-OJ cocktail coming up!
ORANGE
BANANA
What's this supposed to be?
Gaspard
It's a seven-legged horse with a house and a sock on its back. Ridiculous.
Blah blah... my latest work... blah blah blah... big show in New York...
Wonderful, Superb!
What a piece of garbage!
Gaspard
Gaspard
Shush! Not so loud!

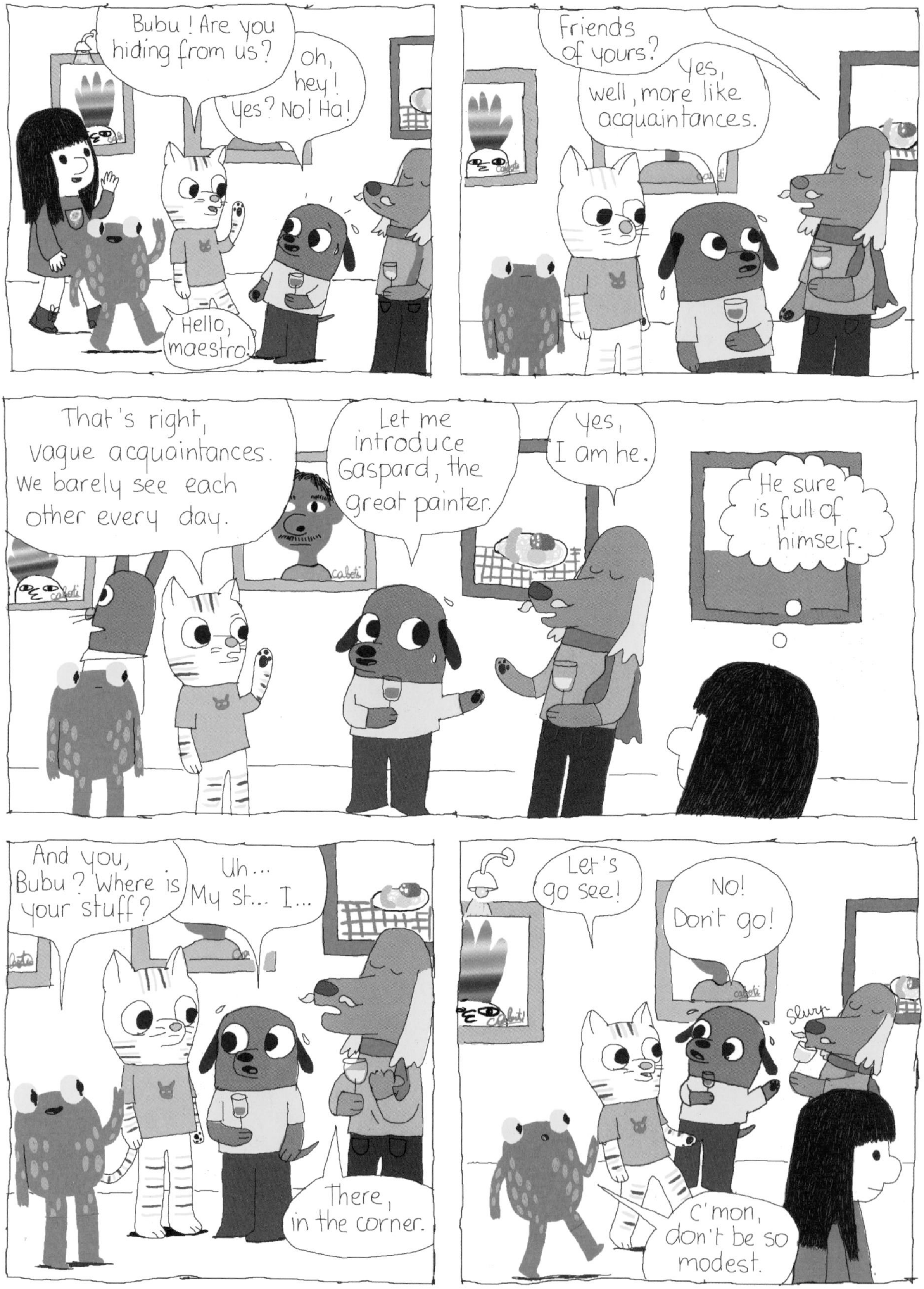
Bubu! Are you hiding from us?
Oh, hey! Yes? No! Ha!
Hello, maestro!
Friends of yours?
Yes, well, more like acquaintances.
That's right, vague acquaintances. We barely see each other every day.
Let me introduce Gaspard, the great painter.
Yes, I am he.
He sure is full of himself.
And you, Bubu? Where is your stuff?
Uh... My st... I...
There, in the corner.
Let's go see!
No! Don't go!
Slurp
C'mon, don't be so modest.

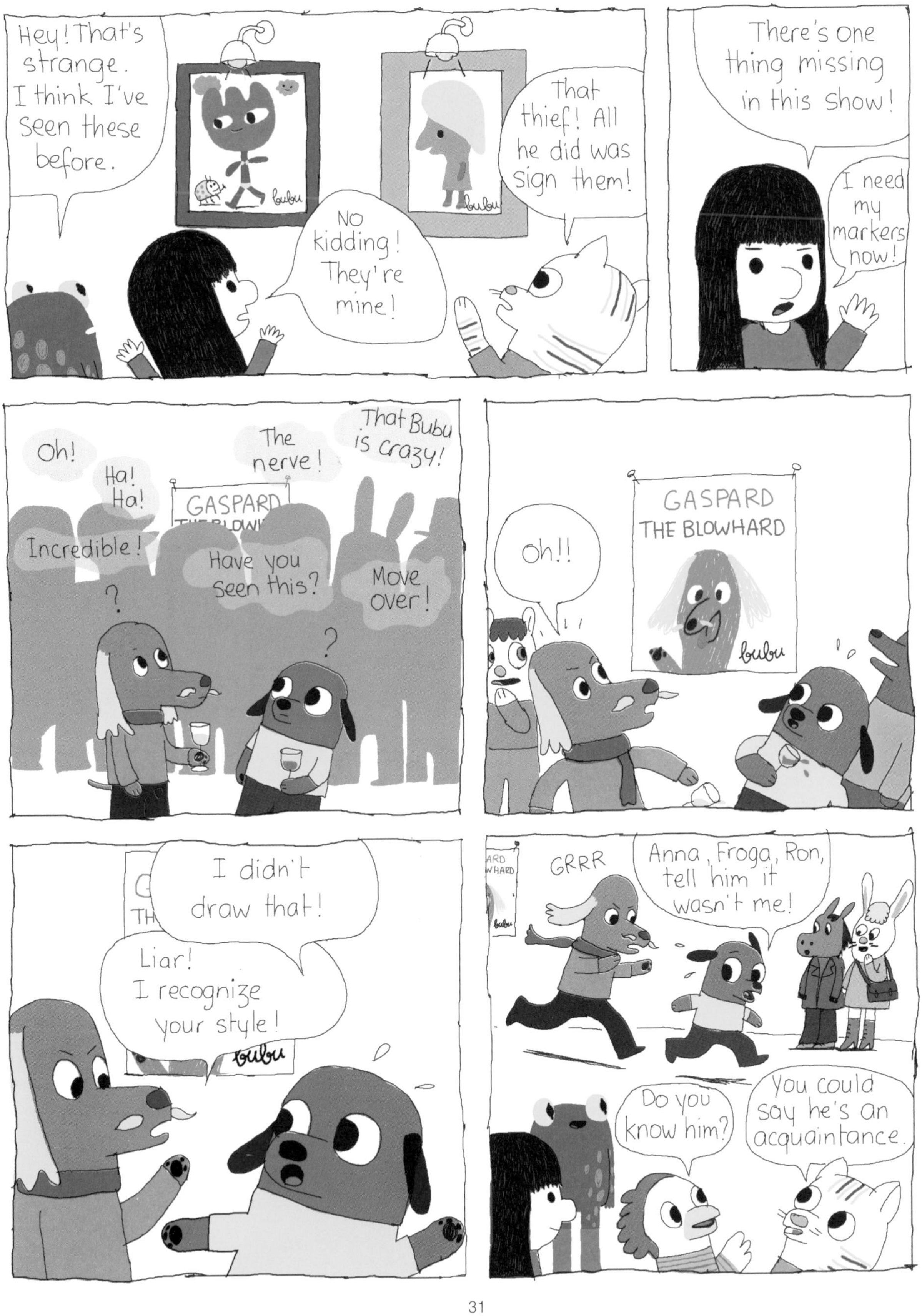
Hey! That's strange. I think I've seen these before.
bubu
bubu
No kidding! They're mine!
That thief! All he did was sign them!
There's one thing missing in this show!
I need my markers now!
Oh!
Ha! Ha!
The nerve!
That Bubu is crazy!
Incredible!
Have you seen this?
Move over!
?
?
GASPARD THE BLOWHARD
Oh!!
bubu
I didn't draw that!
Liar! I recognize your style!
bubu
GRRR
Anna, Froga, Ron, tell him it wasn't me!
Do you know him?
You could say he's an acquaintance.

Anna
RON
BUBU
Froga

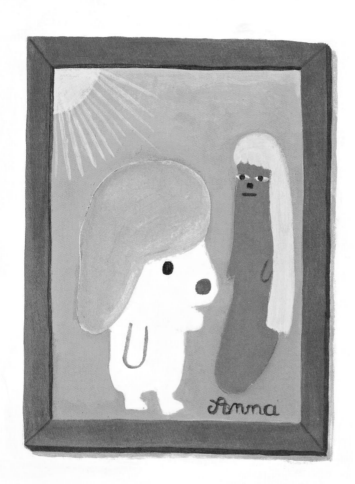

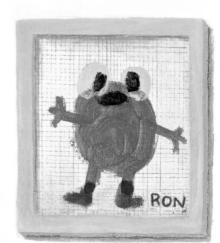

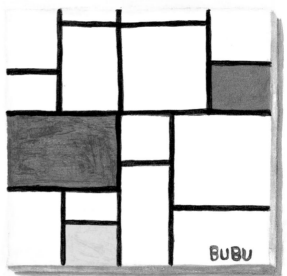

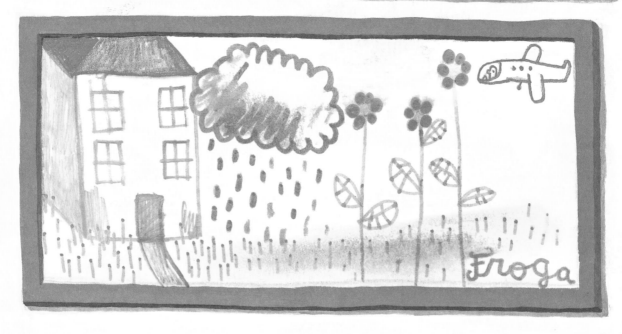

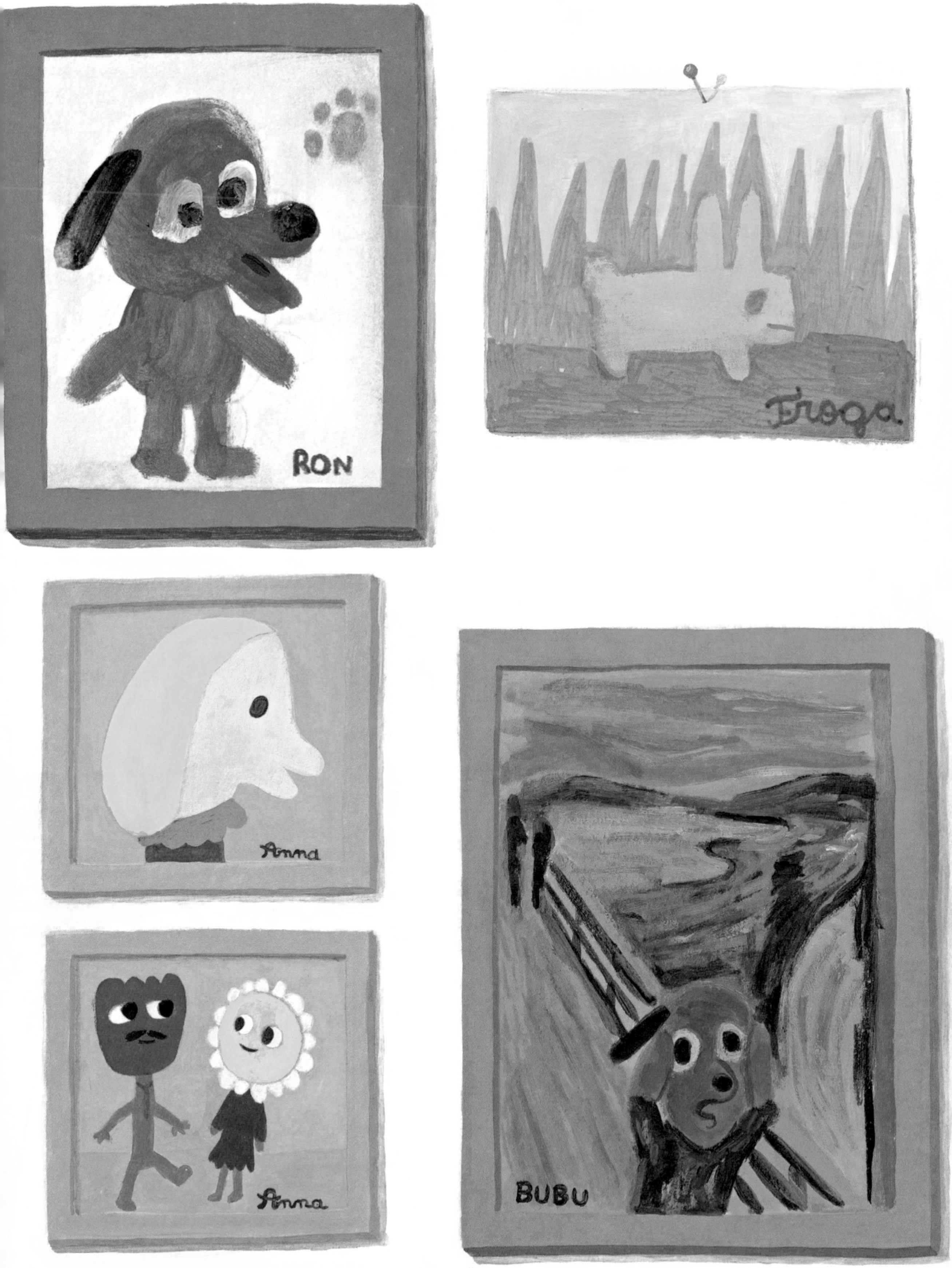
RON
Froga
Anna
Anna
BUBU

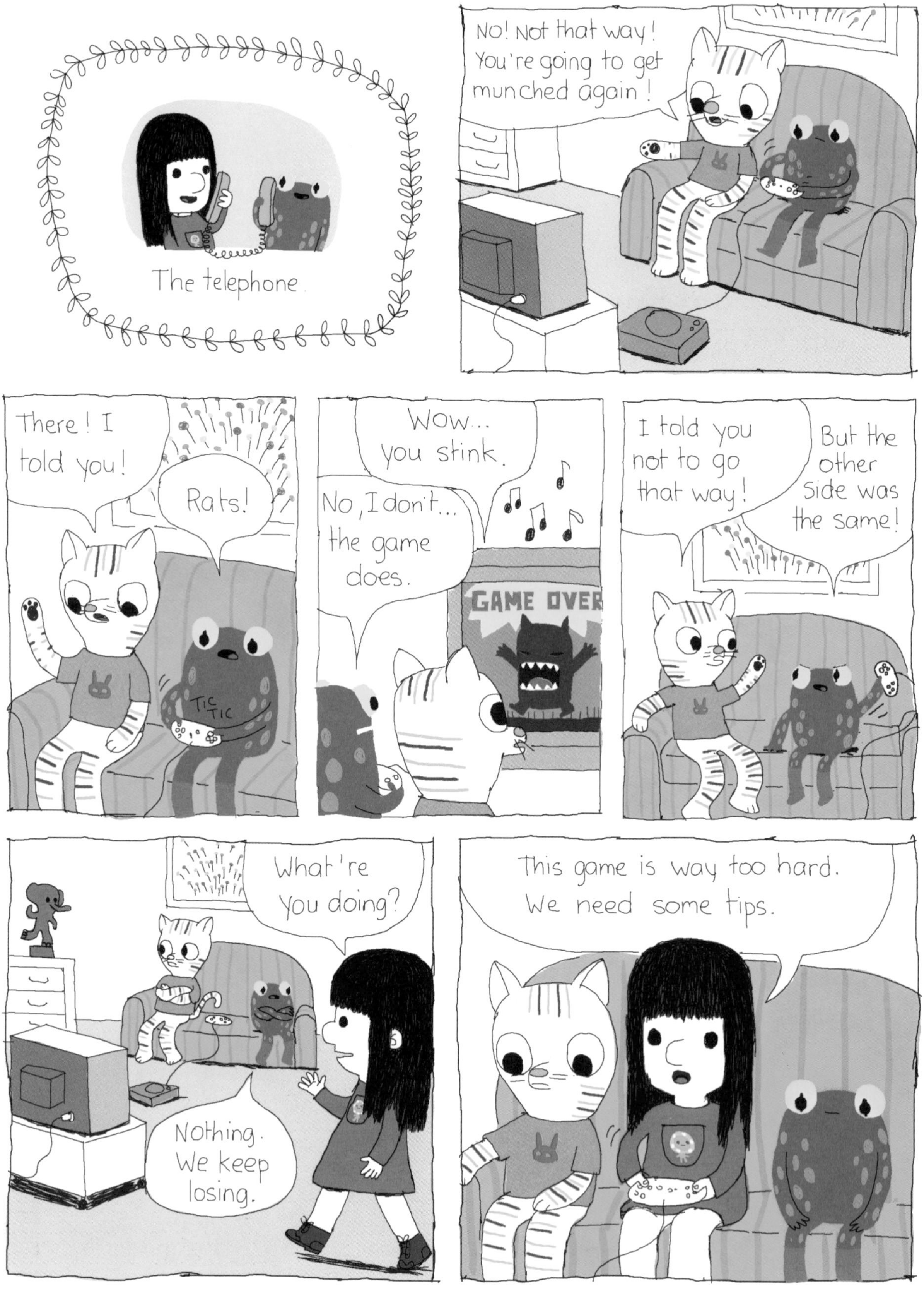

The telephone
No! Not that way! You're going to get munched again!
There! I told you!
Rats!
TIC TIC
Wow... you stink.
No, I don't... the game does.
GAME OVER
I told you not to go that way!
But the other side was the same!
What're you doing?
Nothing. We keep losing.
This game is way too hard. We need some tips.

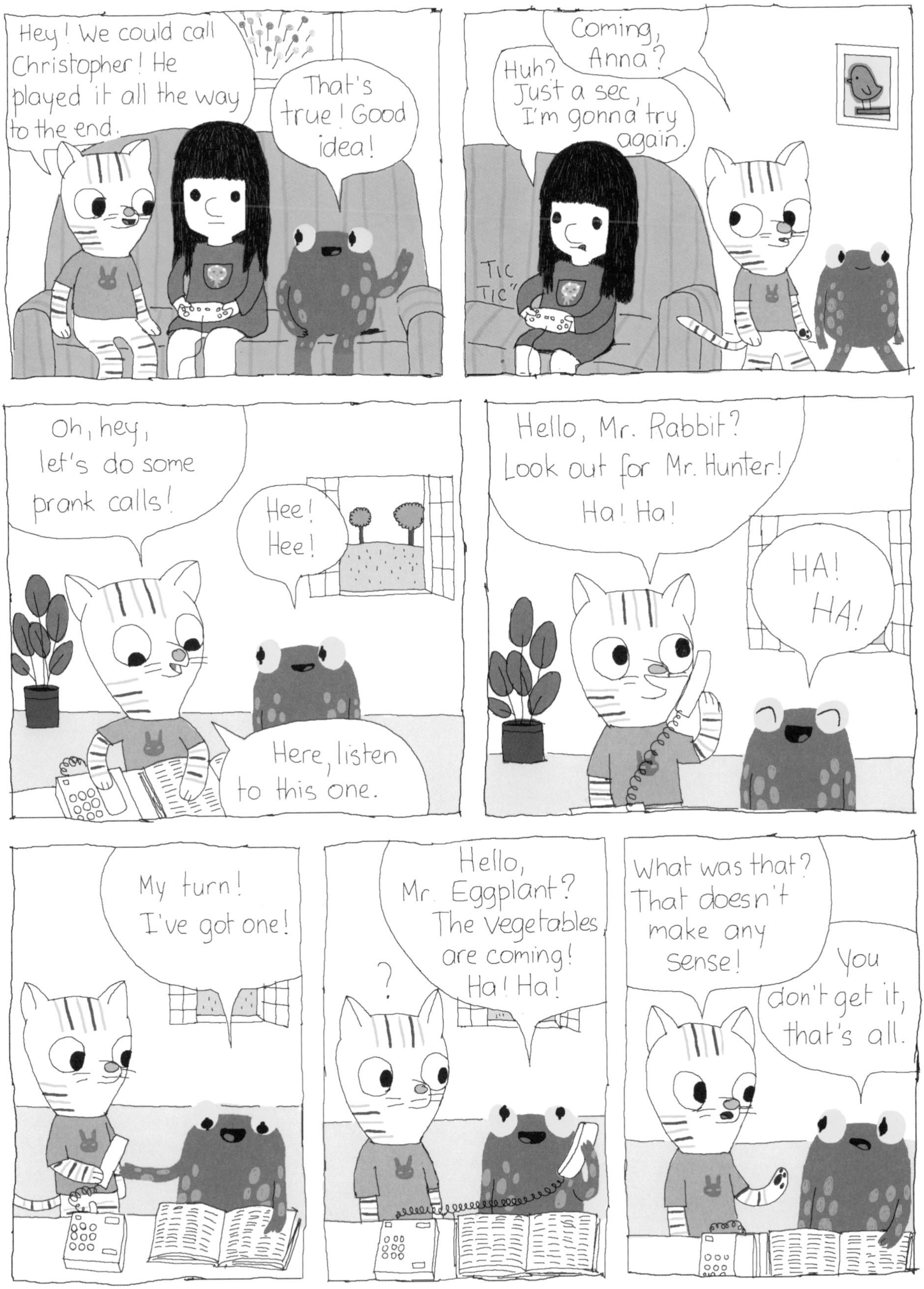
Hey! We could call Christopher! He played it all the way to the end.
That's true! Good idea!
Coming, Anna?
Huh? Just a sec, I'm gonna try again.
TIC TIC
Oh, hey, let's do some prank calls!
Hee! Hee!
Here, listen to this one.
Hello, Mr. Rabbit? Look out for Mr. Hunter! Ha! Ha!
HA! HA!
My turn! I've got one!
?
Hello, Mr. Eggplant? The vegetables are coming! Ha! Ha!
What was that? That doesn't make any sense!
You don't get it, that's all.

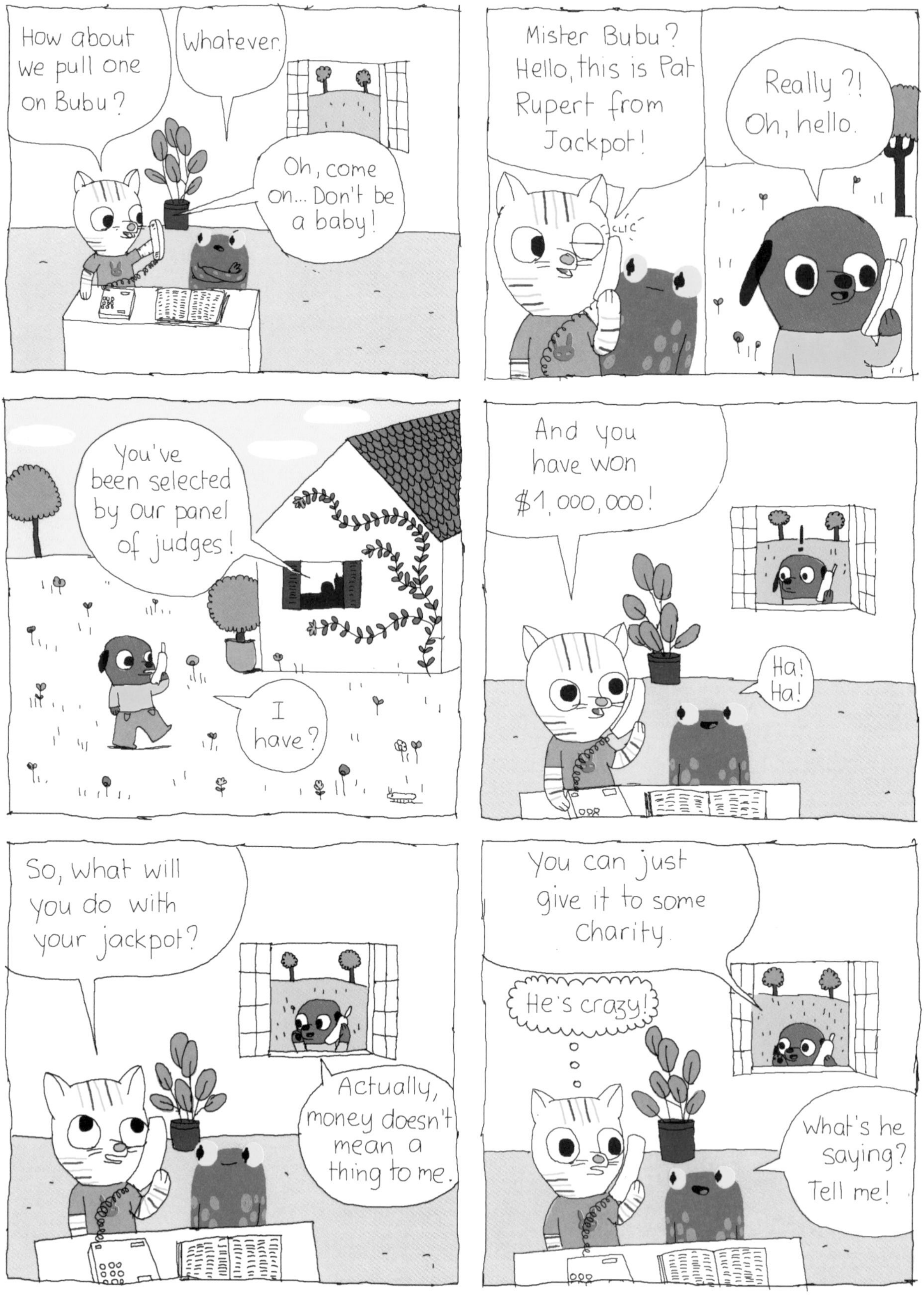
How about we pull one on Bubu?
Whatever.
Oh, come on... Don't be a baby!
Mister Bubu? Hello, this is Pat Rupert from Jackpot!
CLIC
Really?! Oh, hello.
You've been selected by our panel of judges!
I have?
And you have won $1,000,000!
Ha! Ha!
So, what will you do with your jackpot?
Actually, money doesn't mean a thing to me.
You can just give it to some charity.
He's crazy!
What's he saying? Tell me!

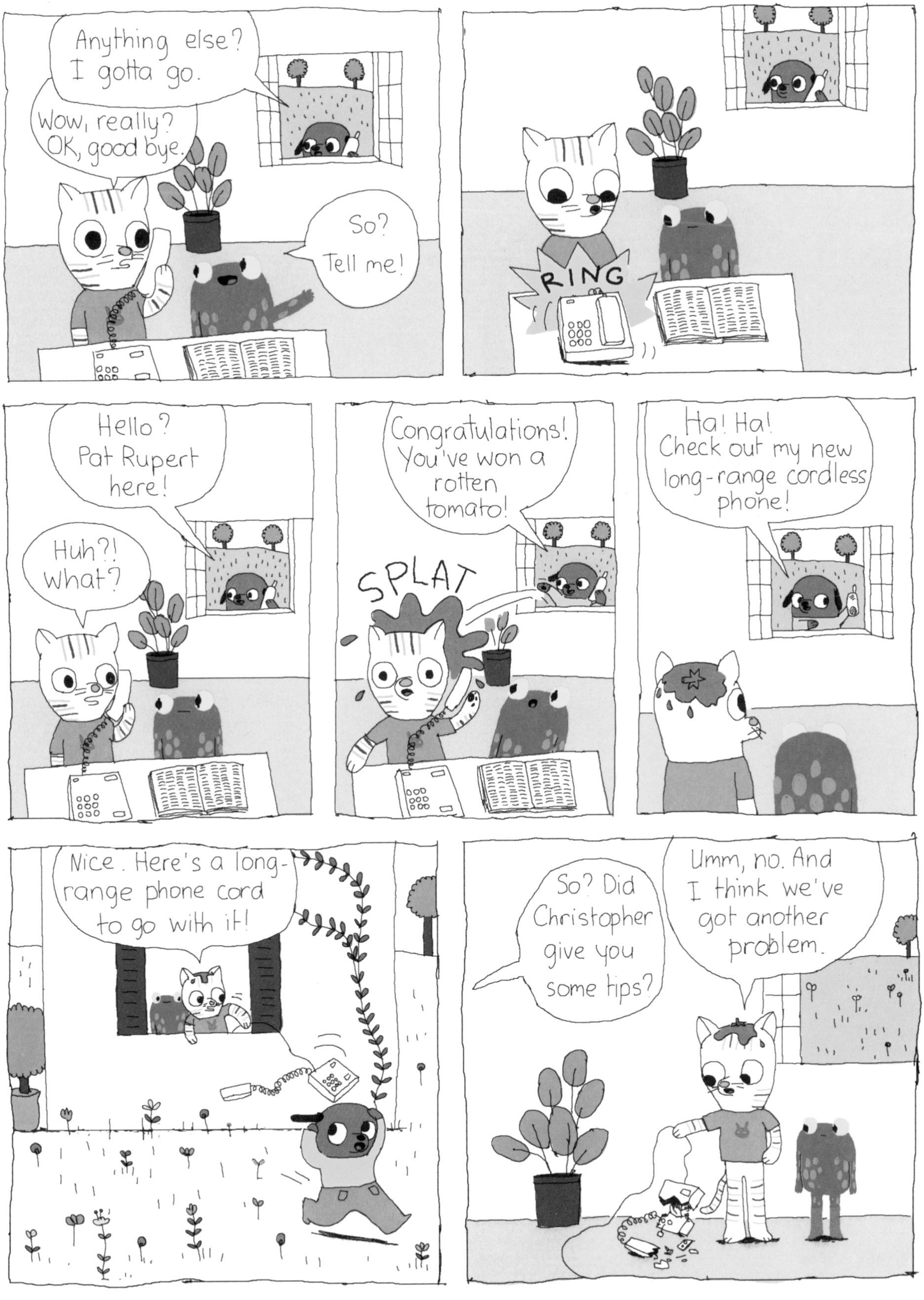
Anything else? I gotta go.
Wow, really? OK, good bye.
So? Tell me!
RING
Hello? Pat Rupert here!
Huh?! What?
Congratulations! You've won a rotten tomato!
SPLAT
Ha! Ha! Check out my new long-range cordless phone!
Nice. Here's a long-range phone cord to go with it!
So? Did Christopher give you some tips?
Umm, no. And I think we've got another problem.

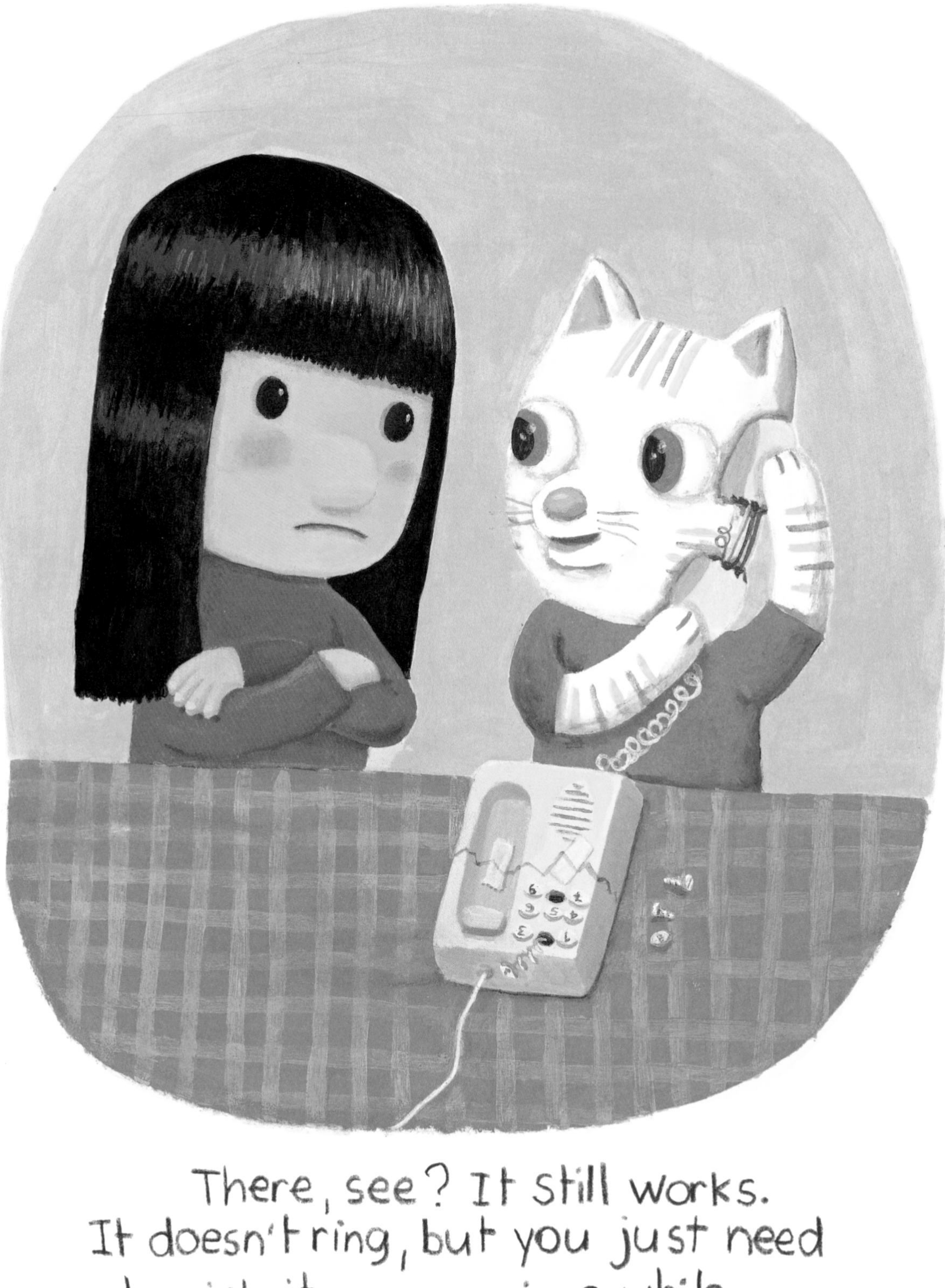

There, see? It still works.
It doesn't ring, but you just need
to pick it up once in a while
to check for calls.

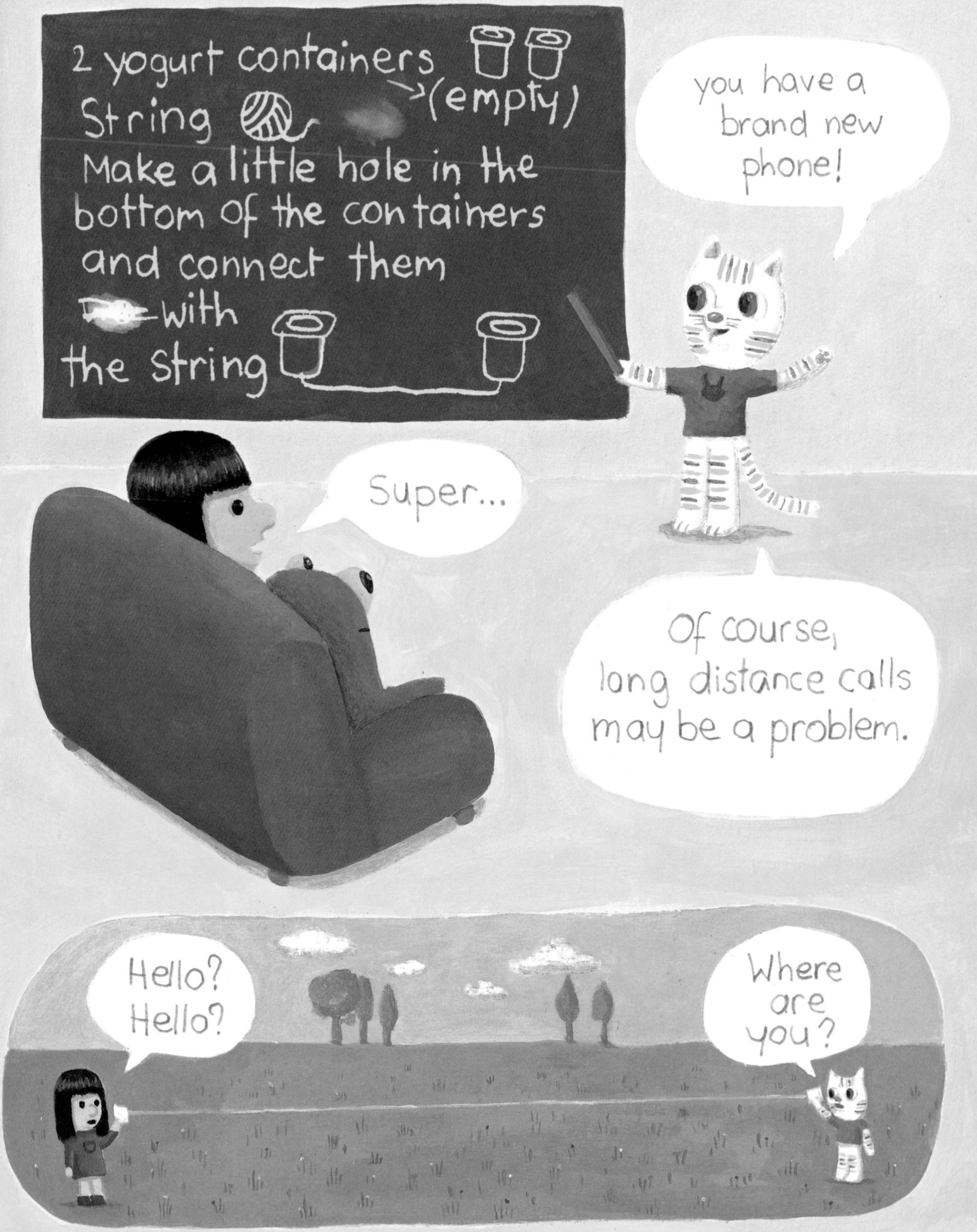
2 yogurt containers
(empty)
String
Make a little hole in the bottom of the containers and connect them with the string
you have a brand new phone!
Super...
Of course, long distance calls may be a problem.
Hello? Hello?
Where are you?

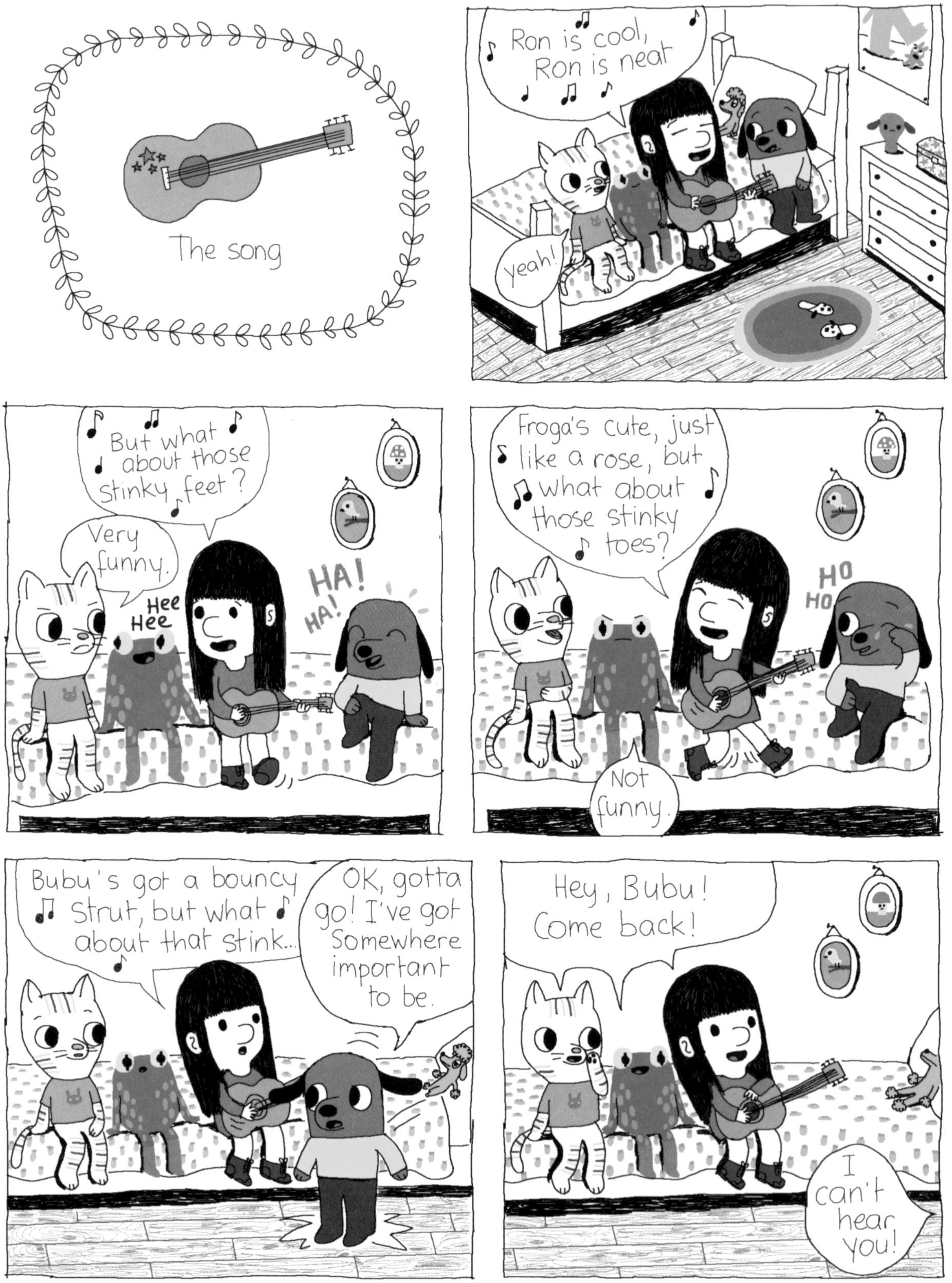
The song
Ron is cool, Ron is neat
yeah!
But what about those stinky feet?
Very funny.
Hee Hee
HA! HA!
Froga's cute, just like a rose, but what about those stinky toes?
HO HO
Not funny.
Bubu's got a bouncy strut, but what about that stink...
OK, gotta go! I've got somewhere important to be.
Hey, Bubu! Come back!
I can't hear you!

Entire contents © 2012 Anouk Ricard. All rights reserved. No part of this book (except small portions for review purposes) may be reproduced in any form without written permission from Anouk Ricard or Drawn & Quarterly. Originally published in French as *Anna et Froga, Tu Veux un Chwingue?* by Éditions Sarbacane. Translated by Helge Dascher with special thanks to John Kadlecek. Thank you to Esme Bale for consulting on this book. Drawn & Quarterly; Post Office Box 48056; Montreal, Quebec; Canada H2V 4S8; www.drawnandquarterly.com. First Hardcover Edition: April 2012. 10 9 8 7 6 5 4 3 2 1. Printed in Singapore. Library and Archives Canada Cataloguing in Publication: Ricard, Anouk; *Anna and Froga: Want a Gumball?* / Anouk Ricard. Translation of: *Anna et Froga, Tu Veux un Chwingue?* ISBN 978-1-77046-070-6; I. Title. II. Title: *Want a Gumball?* PZ7.R63An 2012   jC843'.54   C2011-907517-2. This work, published as part of

Liberté • Égalité • Fraternité
RÉPUBLIQUE FRANÇAISE

grant programs for publication (Acquisition of Rights and Translation), received support from the French Ministry of Foreign and European Affairs and from the Institut français. Cet ouvrage, publié dans le cadre du Programme d'Aide à la Publication (Cession de droits et Traduction), a bénéficié du soutien du Ministère des Affaires étrangères et européennes et de l'Institu français. Drawn & Quarterly acknowledges the financial contribution of the Government of Canada through the Canada Book Fund for our publishing activities and for support of this edition. Distributed in the USA: Farrar, Straus and Giroux; 18 West 18th st; New York, NY 10011; Orders: 888.330.8477. Distributed in Canada by: Raincoast Books; 2440 Viking Way; Vancouver, BC V6V 1N2; Orders: 800.663.5714. Distributed in the United Kingdom by: Publishers Group U.K.; 8 The Arena; Mollison Avenue; Enfield, Middlesex EN3 7NL; Orders: 0208.804.0400.

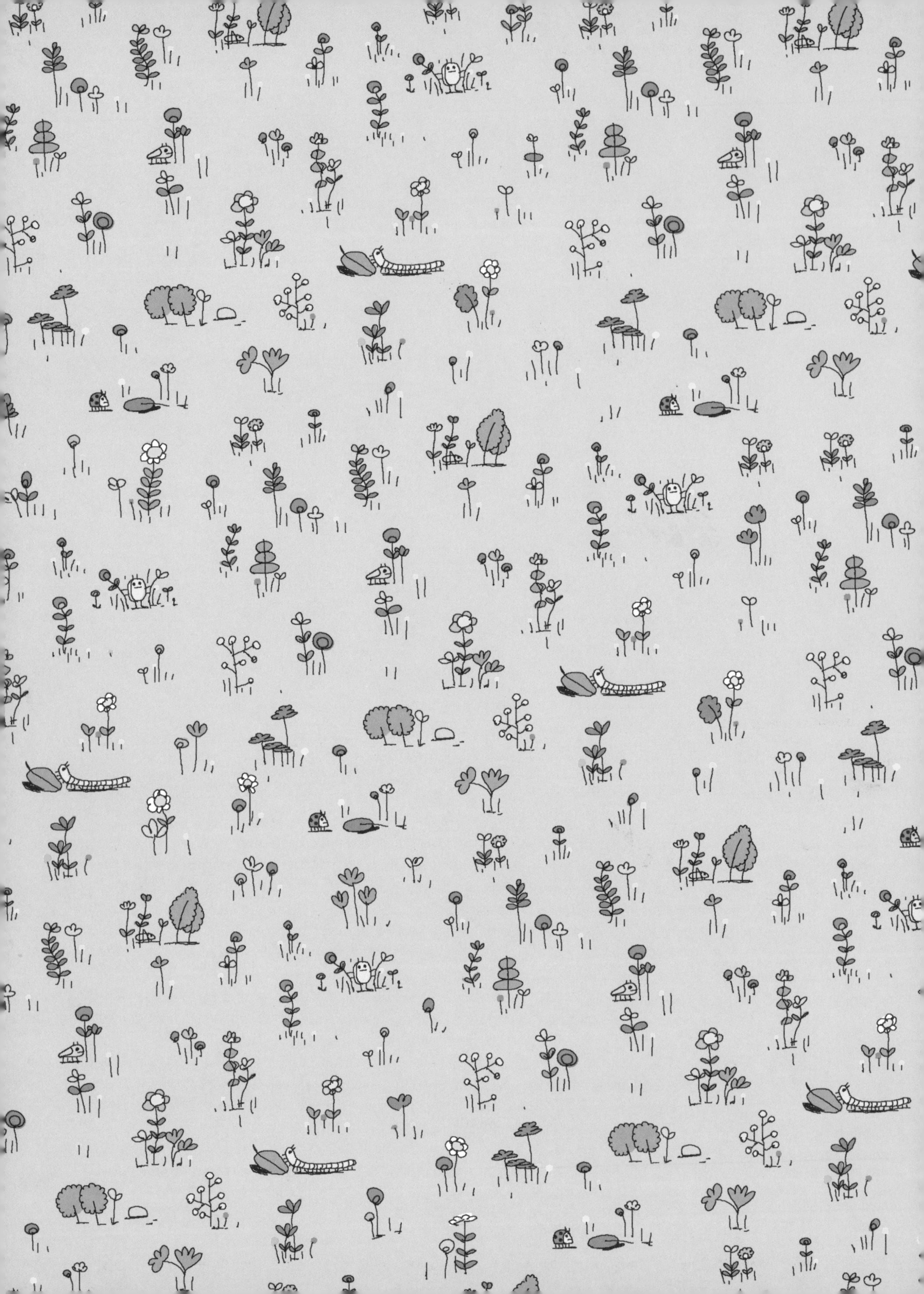